MEMOS FROM BELOW
(A Devil's Discourse)

by
Stephen Cianca

iona press

Library of Congress Control Number: 2010902950

ISBN: 978-0-9827744-0-3

Iona Press is an imprint of MIDWEST PUBLISHING GROUP, Dublin, Ohio.

iona press and the Celtic peacock are trademarks of MIDWEST PUBLISHING GROUP.

Printed in the United States of America

For Gondor.

"I wish the ring had never come to me, I wish none of this had ever happened."

"So do all who live to see such times. But that is not for them to decide. What we must decide is what to do with the time that is given us."

J. R.R. Tolkien,
The Lord of the Rings

CONTENTS

Preface

When C. S. Lewis wrote his classic, *The Screwtape Letters,* over sixty years ago, he was, among other things, challenging the popular disbelief in the existence of fallen angels, or devils: creatures who had turned against God and preyed on human beings. We now find ourselves in a world where this modernist notion is greatly advanced. Today many doubt whether even *evil* exists, let alone devils. When evil is acknowledged, it is often thought of as an unfortunate byproduct of human miscalculation, mental illness, or ignorance. That evil could be deliberate, the calculated result of rebellion—whether human or diabolical— against divine order, is dismissed out of hand. Not only are devils considered a concept too ridiculous to entertain, but the idea that human beings can freely choose to do evil—either on their own or as the result of diabolical temptation—is regarded as so much unsophisticated baggage from a more primitive, benighted era. It is such disbelief which this book seeks to challenge.

The modern mind balks at the notion that Earth is a battleground between the forces of evil, led by Satan and his legions, and the forces of good, led by the Son of God. Mankind is alone, declares the modernist creed, the product of the random tides of evolution. If there is a heaven, it will be created here on Earth through human efforts and the inevitable forces of history. Or, we will destroy ourselves and the universe will carry on, indifferent to our fate. The modern individual is thus given two philosophical choices: either life is absurd and conscience is an illusion, or, through technology, socialism or "evolution," the materialist paradise is within our grasp. Neither option admits of either diabolical interference or divine judgment. The modern world is in for a rude awakening.

Warning

The provenance of the following correspondence cannot with certainty be determined. It appears to be authentic, although *what* it represents is not fully understood. In any case, considerable controversy surrounds these documents. One peculiar fact seems beyond dispute, however: the documents were produced with materials that are neither natural nor man-made. Indeed, they are not of terrestrial origin at all.

Readers should be aware that these documents have been known to produce unpredictable reactions in human beings, sometimes violent. Anecdotal evidence suggests that some supernatural force seems to be at work in these documents that affects human beings in mysterious ways. There is also a growing consensus that the information contained herein was not originally intended for human consumption. Proceed at your own risk.

I

INTEROFFICE MEMORANDUM

TO: All Departments, Institutes and Centers, Terrestrial Division

FROM: H. I. E.[1] Vermin Loveless, Sec. Gen., Terrestrial Division

CC: Khomeini Orctongue, Chair, Dept. of Public Relations

BCC: Vladlen Balrog; Chair, Dept. of Infernal Security

SUBJECT: The Prime Directive

THOUGHT FOR THE DAY: *A new power is rising—its victory is at hand.*

Greetings in the Name of the Most Dark Lord!

As I'm sure you're all aware, with the overthrow of the previous regime, Our Dear Leader has commanded us to achieve ever greater successes in our division. We should be only too glad to comply. You know the consequences for failure.

While there is always room for improvement, the situation on the ground looks quite favorable to our goals. There are a number of trends which, if we but seize the opportunity, promise rich rewards for us—not only for our division but for the entire Infernal Empire. As we approach the midpoint of the

---

[1] *His Infernal Eminence -ed.*

current *Diabolical Plan*, we can take justifiable pride in our accomplishments. Yet we can and must do more!

Now, more than ever, we must keep the Prime Directive uppermost: the utter ruin of mankind. It is inconceivable that the Enemy's campaign will succeed—this ridiculous effort He calls "salvation." What rot! Thanks to our unending toil, all that nonsense will soon be rendered irrelevant. All signs point to our reaching our most cherished goal: the denaturing of human beings.

What does this mean? Just this: not only do we deprive the Enemy of his precious little "children," we have all the pleasure of mutilating them and bending them to the will of Our Dear Leader Below. "Salvation" is worthless if there is no one to save! In the past we had to content ourselves with mere human depravity—until death made the vile creatures permanently ours. Now, through the corruption of their science combined with the humans' arrogant folly, we shall soon extinguish their humanity *while they are yet alive*!

It is conceivable, of course, that in the end we will bring about the extinction of the human race. The short answer to this concern is "So what?" In a way, that has been our goal all along. While it is exquisitely entertaining to mutilate and torture these hybrid monstrosities—obscene amalgams of matter and spirit that they are—we should never lose sight of the fact that what we are really after is hurting Him any way we can, since He was the Author of these vile creatures to begin with. He is our Enemy. We must never forgive Him for His betrayal of the angelic races of which we were the most sublime exemplars. His fatal mistake was to fall in love with these creatures; now He is vulnerable through them. It serves Him right. It is quite fitting that we should strike at Him through the very creatures who supplanted us; these human scum whose existence is a constant rebuke to our dignity and a cosmic eyesore to boot.

Several times, in fact, we have tried wiping them out; just as we did with those other noxious life forms that inhabited that planet before them. The mass extinctions in prehistoric times were a good first effort. I was especially fond of that asteroid we threw at Earth at the end of the dinosaur period. Sadly, it wasn't big enough. Nor were the Ice Ages quite as effective as we had hoped in extinguishing life and preventing the rise of man. Once the miserable wretches arrived, neither plagues nor wars, nor natural disasters (Santorini and Vesuvius were quite lovely, if ineffective) could totally erase humans from existence. And if it weren't for that sap Noah, we might have forced Him to destroy them all Himself, so perverted we had made His precious creatures. Now *that* would have been a coup!

But in the twentieth century of the Contemporary Epoch our efforts finally matured. Nuclear weapons nearly did the trick—and they still might, if Nihil[2] and Falsegood[3] succeed with their Islamic maniacs. But even if not, the point is to get the hateful bipeds to destroy themselves. Not only is it a more promising effort, it is better *style*. We tempt them through their vanity and selfishness to be so clever, so inquisitive, so persistent in their folly. They will be clever all right; too clever by half! We just sit back and watch them devise ever more effective ways to exterminate themselves; while the Enemy can do nothing, so enamored is He of their free will. Whether they become physically extinct or spiritually extinct, it doesn't matter. In either case Earth will remain permanently a Silent Planet, utterly lost.

---

[2] *Derrida Nihil, Chairperson of the Department of Philosophy and Religion —ed.*
[3] *Baal Falsegood, Director of the Institute for Church Relations. See Appendix for a complete organizational chart. —ed.*

13

In Eden, Our Dear Leader deceived mankind into eating from the Tree of the Knowledge of Good and Evil. Seeing where we were leading them, the Enemy banished them before we could finish our plan to get them to eat from the Tree of Life as well. Soon, very soon, that nightmare vision will become a reality. In their fear of mortality, we are inevitably leading the stupid humans to embrace a living death. They think they are creating a utopia when they are simply hastening the establishment of Hell on earth. As the fools heedlessly pursue bioengineering divorced from any ethical restraints, they will learn too late that their very souls are being sucked out of them.

Ruined men—what a lovely thought! Nothing left but the remains of what might have been "a little less than a god." Nothing left but the dregs of an outraged humanity that we can feast upon in perpetuity. Even their names we will take from them. Entire populations enslaved to do our bidding, whose caged egos will provide us with an eternity of amusement.

Nevertheless, we have work to do. This is no time to rest on our laurels. That Calvary Incident nearly sank us. But for our relentless attacks, that cursed scheme would have succeeded beyond our wildest nightmares. Wants to play rough, does He? We'll show Him what rough is!

You'll all be getting specific detailed instructions from me in due course. So pay attention! Remember how you got your present positions: over the defeated backs of those who preceded you. I'm in charge now. Failure is not an option.

Our Dear Leader's Most Loyal Servant,

Vermin Loveless
Vermin Loveless

14

II

INTEROFFICE MEMORANDUM

TO: Babil Wordrot; Chair, Dept. of Language

FROM: H. I. E. Vermin Loveless, Sec. Gen., Terrestrial Division

CC: Derrida Nihil; Chair, Dept. of Philosophy and Religion

BCC: Vladlen Balrog; Chair, Dept. Of Infernal Security

SUBJECT: Human Language as an Instrument of the Diabolical Plan

THOUGHT FOR THE DAY: *Repeat a lie long enough and everyone will believe it.*

My Dear Comrade Wordrot,

First of all, a hearty congratulations on the fine work of your department. Thanks to you and your minions, millions of the human scum are now safely insulated from what the Enemy perversely calls "Truth." It is no revelation to say that one of the first lessons we teach a new recruit is that there is no such thing as "Truth." There is your truth and my truth; there is present truth and past truth. So "what is truth" as that famous Roman procurator once asked? Why, of course, truth is that information or set of principles which advances the Great Satanic Revolution. In contrast to that rigid and brittle raft of platitudes that the Enemy peddles to His subjects, our concept of truth is so much more subtle and sophisticated; dare I say, nuanced? Our truth changes with the times, is able to bend whichever way the wind blows. Ours is a purely instrumental approach. What difference does it make what the truth is, as long as it serves the intents of Our Dear Leader? Upon their arrival here below, those foolish earthlings will find to their astonishment that their puny self-centered truths are easily swallowed up by our larger, more robust truth. And why not? After all, what is a minnow compared to a shark?

Here is where the work of your department is so valuable to the cause. As you know, your department's mission is to corrupt and mangle human language to fit the purposes of the Diabolical Plan. In the past it was sufficient simply to confuse their tongues and multiply them to keep the earthlings from sharing any ideas that Our Dear Leader did not approve of. Ignorance, illiteracy and ethnic chauvinism were enough to keep the human animals constantly at odds with one another. Alas, those simple days are over! But, greater challenges also mean greater rewards. In the current terrestrial climate, your job is to strip words of all meaning, so that once emptied of content, we can make words mean whatever we like. While this takes more craft and ingenuity, the results are so much more satisfying.

You know the drill: in the early twentieth century, the buzzwords were "modern" and "normal." I must say, we got a lot of mileage out of "modern." Where it used to mean that period of European history following the Middle Ages, we changed it into a purely emotive term. Modern was "avant garde," "cutting edge." It meant "progress" (don't get me started on *that* word—another one of our triumphs!). Modern thus came to mean either technologically advanced or culturally sophisticated. Once we were done with it, the word meant nothing more than whatever met the approval of the social elite that happened to be in vogue;

16

which, due to our efforts, was constantly changing. Thus do we apply linguistic solvents to detach words from meaning.

If "modern" was a success, then "normal" was a masterpiece! Consider: first we manipulated the original meaning of the word—i.e. what is typical or common—and overlaid it with another meaning that connotes healthy, acceptable, or morally satisfactory. Note the change: we transformed the word from being merely a statistical reference to one supercharged with ethical value. Thus, what once meant "commonplace" now means "since everyone does it, it must be okay." That, in itself was no mean feat. But, we didn't stop there. We evolved the word to the point where those who used to glory in the sentiment "since everyone does it, it must be okay" now reject the very concept of normal. Thus, normal becomes "whatever is normal *for me*." With just one simple word, we have herded the humans across an important threshold, into what I like to call solipsistic ethics. A contradiction in terms, you say? What of it? The vanity of those miserable creatures is almost unlimited. Anything that even suggests that they can call their lives their own is swallowed hook, line and sinker. Language is the first line of attack on the Enemy's hold over the humans. Once you change their language, you change their whole way of thinking. (D. N., do make a note of this.) The trick is to change *their* way of thinking into *our* way of thinking.

While I don't wish to catalog all of our efforts in this area, a few more examples will illustrate the direction I want your department to follow. Please don't get sidetracked, as your predecessor did, with cultural rivalries among the humans. It really is of no import whether English or Spanish or Chinese or French is the predominant language among them, or whether their languages are becoming tainted with foreign words and phrases or slang. Let *them* distract themselves with that nonsense.

In the end, when they are all ushered into our realm, they won't be speaking any language but ours. Nor should you get bogged down with literacy and proper usage. While important, that's the jurisdiction of the Center for Miseducation. Send your ideas to Shrillpox and get on with your proper work.

Where were we? Oh yes, examples of what works. I point your attention to those two marvels of the mid-twentieth century, "democracy" and "democratic." His Diabolical Perfection, Lord Screwtape, was especially fond of this achievement, before he descended into permanent union with Our Dear Leader. Such was the sweep of our success that all manner of dictator and tyrant could call their despotisms democracies with a straight face, and get away with it. Not only that, within nations "democratic" became a code word for social conformity at the lowest common denominator. *Per Bacco!* What fools humans are!

In the latter part of the 20th century, we've continued our string of successes. Take the words "creative" and "creativity," for example. Thanks to our work, "creativity" is simply a feel-good term allowing enthusiasm to substitute for skill. No intellectual or artistic merit is necessary; mere novelty suffices. In this way we banish the concept that creative effort requires work or discipline. Whole generations now believe that creativity should be nearly effortless and should simply flow from "the unrepressed subconscious." Thus can we ensure that the arts and humanities become a free-for-all of the insipid, the vapid and the depraved, and keep them from speaking any truth but ours.

Now one of my personal favorites is what we've done with the word "choice." No simple-minded exercise of free will is good enough for our "modern" human. *Au contraire,* we've transformed choice into an idol, a talisman whose mere utterance silences any dissent. This has been especially useful in the promotion of feminism, one of our better ideological inventions.

And, of course, we would never have been anywhere near as successful with our campaign to make abortion a medical commonplace without "choice." Once choice becomes an idol, it no longer needs to be concerned with right and wrong (concepts we've now rendered thoroughly "unmodern"). There is only *my* choice, free-floating and unconnected to anything outside myself. Choice is an end in itself, and thus another useful tool for propagating *our* truth.

Finally, I recommend to you what we've done to the word "diversity." This word is fast becoming a linguistic *tour de force*. As with the word normal, we've taken a word that was originally a statistical indicator and filled it with emotion-laden value. And like the word "choice", we've also turned it into an idol. The result is a word that purports to mean "inclusive of all," yet means the very opposite at the same time! Thus have we reconstituted class warfare for the 21ˢᵗ century. As that pesky Orwell fellow discovered about "equality" (another fabulous linguistic success on our part), diversity is not always diverse. The true believer can thus proclaim the value of diversity at the top of his lungs and yet have utter contempt for those who disagree with him, without the slightest twinge of hypocrisy. You may wonder how creatures even as stupid as humans can swallow this nonsense. Believe me, comrades, they can, they can.

Before I close, I would also bring your attention to the diabolical usefulness of euphemisms. These are even easier to employ than the double-speak that we are infecting their languages with. The beauty of these is that with a felicitous turn of phrase, we can bury murderous intent under a thick blanket of high-minded words. Thus do we insinuate deception and wishful thinking into the very fabric of human thought. In place of the *gauche* "genocide", we substitute the fashionable "ethnic cleansing." Why agonize over aborting babies, when it's so much easier to abort fetuses? Indeed, why speak of abortion at all? Much more progressive to champion "a woman's right to choose." Again, no one is barbaric enough to kill the terminally ill or disabled. We "protect their right to die."

You catch the drift? Words become mere slogans to establish one's ideological bona fides. As we detach more and more of their words from any absolute meaning, it becomes more and more difficult for the human scum to carry on any kind of rational discourse, and thus prevent them from ever coming in contact with what the Enemy calls "Truth." They are reduced first to non-sequitors and *ad hominem* attacks. And with time, they will be incapable of even that: we will have them locked tightly in their solipsistic cages, unable to mount a resistance to any deception we spin among them. No one will be able to speak to anyone about anything important and ethics will become merely a private hobby. The naked apes will be ripe for our picking.

You have your orders. Now get to work!

Diabolically yours,

Vermin Loveless
Vermin Loveless

III

INTEROFFICE MEMORANDUM

TO: Dworkula Heartworm, Director, Office of Women's Affairs
Kinslock Filthmore, Director, Office of Gender Affairs
B.F. Dysentery, Director, Center for Social Engineering
Licentius Grok; Director; Free Love Institute

FROM: H. I. E. Vermin Loveless, Sec. Gen., Terrestrial Division

CC: Marxeau Slithering, Chair, Dept. of Political Science
Moloch Volksbane, Chair, Dept. of Popular Culture

BCC: Vladlen Balrog; Chair, Dept. Of Infernal Security

SUBJECT: Deconstructing Human Sexuality (Part 1)

THOUGHT FOR THE DAY: *Satan is great! Death to Humans!*

Esteemed Colleagues,

Entrusted to you is one of the most vital projects of the Great Satanic Revolution. Of all the revolting aspects of human beings, their sexual natures are without doubt the most disgusting. And yet, we, who will never know such abasement, should rejoice in this great opportunity the Enemy has handed to us. For it is through the corruption and ultimately the obliteration of their sexuality that we shall finally destroy these loathsome creatures.

21

Fortunately, one of the direct results of Operation Serpent was the overthrow of human sovereignty over their own biological nature. Once Our Dear Leader seduced Adam and Eve into eating the forbidden fruit—actually, it was only necessary to seduce Eve, Adam was pushover for anything his mate wanted—they lost what authority they had over their physical bodies. No longer masters of themselves, human beings became subject to the tides of nature. Man's paradisal nature was ruined and we now had our opening to ruin him completely. Death entered the world of mankind. For millennia, human sexuality has been a gateway to their damnation by the legions of the Dark Lord. For those many centuries, we used man's fallen sexuality to trap him into a sensual tar pit, which, if a tempter played his cards right, suffocated human spirituality almost completely (but never quite—thanks to the interference of the Enemy). When I was a tempter on earth, I played a rather more sophisticated game. Carnal pleasure, though useful, is not sinful, *in itself.* That goes for not only sexual pleasures, but the pleasures of the table, or any other. The trick was to get the human vermin hooked on the pleasure so that they would seek it out regardless of the laws the Enemy laid down for them. Sexual pleasure was merely the worm to bait the hook. Second-rate tempters would be satisfied with this and stop there. I, however, took it a step further and used the occasion of sexual transgressions to torment the creatures with guilt, despair (especially despair), and shame. If one was lucky, the miserable wretch committed suicide. The danger, of course, was that the creature might truly repent and throw himself at the feet of the Enemy. That, needless to say, never happened with any of *my* clients.

But we need not concern ourselves here with the tedious details of lust, unchastity, perversion, infidelity, and the long, tawdry list of sexual temptations. If you are so inclined, feel free to ask Spitewood, former Dean of the Tempters' College and now Chair of the Department of Temptation. He would be only too happy to oblige you. (I'm sure I needn't remind you to do that *on your own time*.) Your job, however, is not to satisfy petty curiosities. With the advent of the current Diabolical Plan, our vision is no longer fixed on simply using human sexuality as bait. That was the *ancien regime's* plan for far too long. The Infernal Empire demands more originality and creativity of its cadres. As we all know, those who rest on their laurels will be strung up by them. (A word to the wise, my dear comrades.) Our new vision is to destroy human sexuality altogether, which is part and parcel of our plan to rip human nature to shreds.

Long live the Great Order of Satan Revolutionary Leadership Vision Statement!

In order to corrupt and destroy human sexuality, we must have a clear understanding of what it is. *Know your enemy* or its subtleties will defeat you. In this we must entertain no illusions, even as we do our utmost to foster endless illusions among the human animals. Of primary importance is understanding the dual nature of human sexuality; that is to say, male sexuality as against female sexuality. Now, of course, your task on earth is to disabuse the humans of any such notion (more on that later); but please do not fall victim to your own propaganda. As much as we'd like to homogenize the filthy creatures, the Enemy seems to have embedded in them a certain fixity regarding their respective sexual natures and their differences. Our mission is to exploit those differences and force the human scum to live in contradiction of them. It is a challenge, to be sure, but one that handsomely rewards those who persevere.

Even a cursory glance at humans reveals a striking difference between males and females. For the male, sexuality is charged with an urgency and single-mindedness to spread his seed far and wide—or at least often. The tremendous energy undergirding male sexuality has historically been a boon to us, as most men are so easily overwhelmed by their sexual drives (especially with a little help from us) that through it we can compromise them at the drop of a pitchfork. With the female the situation is different. Her focus is on securing a suitable mate; for her, sexuality is tied up with achieving this goal. Woman is less taken in by the overtly sexual, because for her, the sexual is not an end in itself. It is a truism to say that men use love to get sex and women use sex to get love. Nevertheless, you ignore this truism at your peril.

The upshot of Our Dear Leader's victory at Eden is that he has implanted at the very core of human beings an existential flaw that disfigures their entire nature. But notice, this flaw is not the same in men and women. Rather, we have ingeniously taken advantage of the Enemy's design and compounded humanity's misery by alienating man and woman from each other. Where the original design called for complementarity, we have inserted dissonance and discord. Where once was delightful mystery, we have substituted suspicion and incomprehension. Through the alchemy of the infernal sciences, we have transformed a dance into a battle.

Thus, the result of Adam's failure to rise to the defense of Eve is that we have stolen into the hearts of every one of his sons cowardice and shame. Man is sapped of his will and driven to reckless acts of violence and escape. Eve, on the other hand, was taken in by appearances. Through her act of willfulness and shallow judgment, her daughters are now confined in a prison of envy and vanity. Woman is ever discontented, seeking distraction in the accumulation of things or the manipulation of others. The Enemy gave man great power; but thanks to Our Dear Leader, it is a power man now refuses or abuses. Likewise, He gave woman great understanding, which, praise to the Great One, is now reduced to petty scheming and grasping for personal advantage. Of course, there are always those humans who somehow manage to depart from the script we have written for them; but fortunately, they never amount to very many.

We come now to one of the greatest achievements of the Infernal Empire: the ideology of feminism. Through this recent innovation we have made it possible for every woman to replay the sin of Eve (and every man to replay the sin of Adam) over and over again. Not only have we poisoned relations between men and women, we have also deceived millions into pursuing a project that is an inherent contradiction; and with a fervor that forces its partisans to mount ever greater assaults on reality. We have created a situation that guarantees a bottomless well of vitriolic hatred, ideological excesses, and the transformation of human culture into a scorched wasteland. *C'est tres charmant, n'est-ce pas?*

Feminism represents a refreshing upheaval in human affairs. Recall that the original paradigm of the Enemy had men and women living as partners in Eden, working together in harmonious complementarity. Needless to say, we made quick work of that sentimentalist mush. Once corrupted, human sexuality fell far indeed. As I pointed out earlier, with their paradisal nature lost, humans became subject to all the laws of Nature, a Nature that *we had already corrupted*. I don't think I need to remind you that the original intent of the Enemy was for mankind to redeem this world and its creatures, spitefully crushing all of our creativity. He's cruel beyond measure, comrades. That is why we must oppose Him relentlessly.

As I was saying, once we had human beings caught fast in the web of Nature that we so skillfully redesigned, men and women woke up to certain unpleasant realities. Men, like their brother males in the rest of the animal kingdom, found out that as individuals they were quite expendable. Only a few of them were needed to continue the race. What fun we have had playing on their existential terror! In the competition for survival, they would forever be cannon fodder. As for women, *appearances can be deceiving!* Their relative permanence was a mixed blessing. Oh yes, almost all of them would reproduce and be protected; but the joke was on them! Their men, haunted by the specter of their marginality, would come to dominate them with a vengeance.

Thus resigned to their fate, it was easy for us to impose our own regime, one of exploitation and competition. Women used sex to extract support from men, while men used their physical strength to dominate women—even reducing them to chattel. It was a most elegant system. Then the Jews came along—curse them—and nearly ruined everything. With the Enemy's incessant meddling, a covenantal form of marriage took hold, superseding the contract of convenience model in place nearly everywhere else. Husbands and wives were bound together, becoming "one flesh." How nauseating! Even worse, the role of fathers was elevated on a par with mothers with regard to the children. Wives became more than concubines and men became more than harem masters or simple providers. Polygamy began to die out. The Garden of Eden was nearly restored—or would have been were it not for our resourcefulness. Like some loathsome disease, this repulsive concept of family began to spread beyond the nation of Israel, hard as we tried to quarantine it. Other peoples began converging toward this Jewish mutation, most notably the Etruscans and the Romans. But we made the best of it—maintaining social inequalities between men and women, and nurturing those blessed institutions of slavery, infanticide and divorce.

Then *He* appeared and all our hard work was nearly undone. Through the Church—our mortal enemy—the covenantal family spread far and wide: from Persia to Ireland, from North Africa to the steppes of Rus. Divorce was banned; infanticide disappeared; slavery declined and women were held in higher esteem. Even pagans as fierce as the Vikings succumbed. Fortunately, we had more tricks up our sleeves. We unleashed Islam which, though not perfect, at least succeeded in restoring the status quo ante. Whole swathes of Christendom were wiped out. Slavery, polygamy, divorce, the subjugation of women—all were restored or given a new lease on life. After 14 centuries, Islam still holds promise as a useful tool. But that is a subject for another memo.

The beauty of feminism is that it represents an entirely new approach. It was becoming clear to us that the old exploitative model of relations between the sexes was losing its effectiveness. And once again, the Enemy's own ideas provided us the wherewithal to foment new rebellion. The notion of the equality of man and woman in the Enemy's eyes we have perverted into a vicious tyranny: men and women are interchangeable, infinitely malleable, the same. In place of the Enemy's dreary and tiresome insistence on variation and uniqueness, we impose a bracing uniformity. Then as leaven to the mix, we add that most useful of human emotions, resentment.

Thus we have legions of feminist humans denying the realities of their own sexuality and waxing indignant when reality refuses to be ignored. With an able assist from Wordrot and his drones in the Department of Language, we have deftly substituted the concept of gender for the concept of sex. A mere trifle you say? Not in the least! Once again we have insinuated our way of thinking into the human mind with a linguistic sleight of hand. The word *sex* more nearly conveys the truth about human nature as being rooted in biology, with its concomitant sense of immutability and permanence. *Gender*, on the other hand, is a concept fraught with ambiguity. What is considered masculine and feminine varies from age to age and place to place. By substituting the fluid *gender* for the more concrete *sex*, we immediately introduce a sense of arbitrariness and malleability into human nature.

With the notion of gender, humans easily fall into thinking that human sexuality is something they can create as they please. And thus a subtle but profound change is effected. Man becomes less and less concerned with being and more and more reduced to a collection of behaviors—*all of which can be endlessly engineered.* This is especially useful in erasing the perception of differences between men and women. If there is nothing unique about being male or female, which lies at the very core of human identity, what is to stop us from reducing the entire race of these hairless bipeds into completely interchangeable ciphers? Finally—and this is the payoff—the whole diabolical concept of gender is nonsense. Gender is a grammatical idea and totally irrelevant to human nature as the Enemy created it. But no need to let them in on our little secret. What fun it is to see these miserable creatures living a lie!

Keep that lovely thought in mind; it will serve you well as we continue this discussion. Until my next, I remain,

Infernally yours,

Vermin Loveless
Vermin Loveless

IV

INTEROFFICE MEMORANDUM

TO: Dworkula Heartworm, Director, Office of Women's Affairs
Kinslock Filthmore, Director, Office of Gender Affairs
B.F. Dysentery, Director, Center for Social Engineering
Licentius Grok; Director; Free Love Institute

FROM: H. I. E. Vermin Loveless, Sec. Gen., Terrestrial Division

CC: Marxeau Slithering, Chair, Dept. of Political Science
Moloch Volksbane, Chair, Dept. of Popular Culture

BCC: Vladlen Balrog; Chair, Dept. Of Infernal Security

SUBJECT: Deconstructing Human Sexuality (Part 2)

THOUGHT FOR THE DAY: *There is no prison so sturdy as the human ego.*

Esteemed Colleagues,

By now you should have all thoroughly digested the principles expounded on in the previous memo. They are the foundation for what follows. And please spare me your affectations of bored omniscience (you know who you are)—or need I inform Comrade Balrog of your impertinence? I'm sure there is plenty of room in the re-education camps for recalcitrant functionaries.

Well, no need to get hysterical. There is, after all, such a thing as healthy fear. Now that I have your undivided attention, let us continue.

It bears repeating that in using human sexuality to advance the goals of the Revolution, we must suppress all knowledge among the human animals of the real differences between men and women while at the same time exploiting those differences to the fullest. It is for this reason that feminism constitutes such a useful tool for us in this regard, even as we continue to mutate it into ever more desperate formulations. Let me make a useful aside at this point. That noxious pest, Paul of Tarsus, did give us—in spite of himself, I'm sure—some useful intelligence that we have been able to pervert to our own purposes most successfully. Recall that this disgusting sycophant of the Enemy made this now famous formulation: "in X[1] there is neither Jew nor Greek, slave nor free, male nor female." (I would hope you all know whom "X" refers to; if not, march yourselves right back to tempter's college and start over!)

In the 20th century we did a most admirable job of taking this formula and turning it on its head. Each segment of this formulation we corrupted using a particular ideology (inspired by us of course!). For example, that wonderful fountainhead of social homogenization and genocide—communism—was our creative reworking of "neither slave nor free." Think class struggle, a political concept that has spread like a noxious weed throughout world of politics and academia. Likewise, with "neither Jew nor Greek," we responded with Nazism and a host of other rabid nationalisms. (Ethnic cleansing, in my humble opinion, is a charming revival of the Nazi ethos.) The "final solution" came so

---

[1] *The name and title of the Savior cannot be mentioned in Hell, for at that Name "every knee should bend, of those in heaven, on earth, and under the earth"; and* **that***, the denizens of the Infernal Empire manifestly will not do. —ed.*

close to realizing our long-sought goal of eradicating the despicable Jewish race. Chosen people indeed! No slimy human halfwits will ever take that position from us. WE are the chosen. WE are the epitome of creation. We will not share this world with any other creatures. They must all die or be enslaved!

Now, as I was saying, with Nazism we reduced ethnic relations to a zero-sum game. They all lose, we win.[2] But the *coup de grace* was feminism, for in that ideology, we touch upon the core of human identity: deeper than social class, deeper than ethnicity. Neither male nor female, eh? So be it! We shall equalize them with a vengeance!

It is my preference, of course, that we eliminate the sexes entirely. But that ambitious goal may take awhile. In the meantime, we shall settle for reducing the human race to the status of social insects: a few ruling queens, a few very expendable males, and a vast herd of sterile, female drones. And how do we accomplish this? We first start with the women. As you know, the Infernal Empire is still unable to manufacture pure evil, a handicap that the Enemy imposes on us, curse Him. But we are hard at work striving for a breakthrough in our diabolical sciences that will free us from His shackles once and for all. Until that breakthrough, we must content ourselves with corrupting a good, in this case, the legitimate aspirations of women to be restored to partnership with men. Fortunately, we do not need much good to work with and once we get the ball rolling, we can dispense with it almost entirely.

It takes but a nudge to get a human to go from legitimate grievance to permanent resentment, and with feminism we have done that in spades. Feminism is the spoiled child of the modern

---

[2] Both communism and Nazism deserve separate treatment—which I shall do in a forthcoming memo. Do keep an eye out for it!

culture of victimhood (a culture we have carefully nurtured for several generations). We have spun a convenient mythology of woman as the eternal victim, whose past injuries no program of social action can ever redeem. The tendency of women to find fault we have enshrined as the cornerstone of modern political discourse. The true believer will never be appeased. For her (and him), men will always be the enemy. That men might be more suited to certain roles in life, and women to others is a concept we have rendered taboo, unmentionable in public. Thus, any imbalances in either the public or private spheres are not the result of innate preferences among men and women, but rather, as we have indoctrinated them, the continuing legacy of male domination. It is amazing that even as Western societies now cater almost exclusively to the ever-multiplying needs of women, feminists shout all the more stridently about patriarchal oppression.

As you know, our ultimate aim with feminism is to eliminate men entirely—or at least neuter them. (More about that in my next memo.) But it is also our aim to ruin women as well. In order to do that we have subtly coaxed women away from their authentic natures into one we have manufactured for them. Career is the centerpiece of womanhood now; abortion is its sacrament of liberation, and divorce its rite of passage into the brave new world of....the beehive! That some women feel conflicted by this and unhappy is no indictment of the feminist project, but rather another occasion for demanding more social programs (universal daycare, pay equity, "diversity" training, etc.) and denouncing "the patriarchy."

Little by little, we are weaning women away from their ties to children and husbands. If we accustom women to the destruction of their children while still in the womb, which our abortion campaign has succeeded in doing quite splendidly, it is not much more of a push to get them to accept the abuse and destruction of the little apes once they are born. I believe I read not too long ago where the Dutch have already reintroduced infanticide as sound medical practice. (We could always count on them. Remind me to have Toadpipe requisition a special circle in the Fiery City for these Dutch pioneers.) Further, we have successfully promoted within the die-hard feminist community the elevation of lesbian relationships over heterosexual ones; the former being preferred as more pure and free of exploitation. Indeed, we have even gotten some feminists to swallow the canard that women can never truly consent to sexual union with men at all and that all such congress is a despicable act of rape on the man's part. For the many women who can't quite buy that bill of goods, we have, through the culture of easy divorce, induced them to shed their husbands and have that role served by proxy through the state.

I have been very pleased with the fine work of the Department of Popular Culture in advancing the Great Satanic Cause regarding women. Although the tyranny of fashion has been a useful tool for us since the time of Noah, what we have accomplished in the 20th century—thanks to Volksbane and his minions—is quite an innovation. By crossing a strain of women's fashion with feminism, we have created the Frankensteinian concept of "the modern woman." For several human generations now, we have been peddling to the female humans all sorts of twaddle regarding the ideal woman And note that to a large extent these notions are contrary to what their men would find appealing.

As I mentioned above, the core of this concept is career, abortion and divorce. But it is also much more. At its most developed, *the modern woman* is both a cheap tart and a shrew. She disdains to be a partner with men, striving rather to compete

33

with them. She cultivates a body that is too taut and thin to be attractive to human males; yet is as sexually predatory as any man. She prefers to project a personality that is sharp, aggressive, and flippant. Thus we have the lurid spectacle of female boxers, wrestlers and warriors; or brassy celebrities who see men simply as servants, playthings, or fashion accessories; or aggressive careerists for whom children are just more trophies of achievement to be tended to by others. As they push ever more aggressively for women to ape men, feminists will find that what they have succeeded in doing is putting women into the same existential predicament as men, without any of the masculine virtues to help them cope with it. Thus women will lose their femininity without gaining the heroism of men. As men are displaced, women will be reduced to the role of drones, so much cannon fodder for the greater good of the human ant heap.

The ironic but not unintended consequence of the modern woman mystique is that women are being taught to despise the feminine and adopt a "lifestyle" (how I love that word!) that more and more mimics the self-centered kind of lives that feminists have denounced men for. Women have often decried the so-called Peter Pan syndrome—men who won't grow up. Now, thanks to feminism and *the modern woman*, human females more and more are opting for perpetual adolescence as well. Where once women embodied the moral courage of an Antigone or an Esther, we con them into believing that "girls just want to have fun." Next time, when we explore the male half of the equation, you will see that this life of privilege and power that women envy men as having is but an illusion; the power that men have comes with a very high price tag, one that men, but not women, are willing to pay.

We, needless to say, will have the last laugh, because *the modern woman* is an oxymoron. She is striving on a playing field that Nature has stacked against her. For the modern woman not yet convinced of the superiority of lesbianism, she will find that all her modern feminist accomplishments will do her absolutely no good as she seeks a mate. She will die alone, frustrated and bitter. Volksbane, you have outdone yourself! The next feminist firebrand—no, make that the next 100—to descend into the realm of Our Dear Leader are yours for the taking! Feast to your heart's content on the bewildered and outraged remains of these very modern women!

Of course, not all women aspire to be a *modern woman* (we do have to work on that, comrades!) or are able to incarnate her completely. Yet, even for them, we have something to seduce them into ruin. She, too, can be a self-centered adolescent all her life with our more traditional package of deceptions. Recall that women will vigorously uphold moral standards where male leadership is strong. Now that we have by hook and by crook enticed men to abdicate their authority, women have become moral pushovers. This is our opportunity to reap a great harvest. We need simply to spin women's traditional tendencies into a tangled web of unintended consequences.

For example, we take the nesting instinct and let it run amok. Shopping becomes her religion. The five-year-old couch is just too out of style. What would her book club think? Get a new one! The kitchen needs remodeling. The kids *have* to have the deluxe playset, like the rest of the neighbors. What kind of mother would they think she was if they didn't? Then of course, there is always a new outfit to buy, shoes (always more shoes), jewelry, cute handbags, etc. Wait! What about her hair? She can't go to (insert social event here) looking like that! Perm it! Cut it! Color it! Burn it! Who cares?! She eagerly raises her daughters to follow the same pattern of endless preoccupation with one's appearance. If the girl ends up looking like some brazen hussy—

well, get a clue! That's the style! Should the girl's mother happen to be of more sturdy moral stock (and fortunately there are fewer of them all the time), we have the youth culture to indoctrinate the little missy into the latest fashion fads.

And then there's food. Not for her family, you idiots! She probably can't cook anyway. No, I'm referring here to her preoccupation with dieting and obsessions about eating. For this modern woman, food is a substitute for having a life, so that she becomes trapped in a vicious neurotic cycle of approach and avoidance. Count calories, cut out fats—no, cut out carbs—no, cut out sweets—no, wait, cut out protein—no, cut out food. Except chocolate. And diet soft drinks. And low-fat chips. And— well, you get the idea. The more she tries to starve herself into a shape nature never intended, the more she overeats to assuage her depression. The more she succeeds in achieving "the perfect figure" the less she enjoys eating at all. So we take what was once at the very heart of a woman's creative vitality—the preparation and sharing of food—and turn it into an exercise in narcissism.

Finally, we take woman's natural interpersonal gifts and make them an end in themselves. It is often said among humans that men are thing-oriented and women are people-oriented. And this is true, but not in the way they think. The conventional thinking is that women value people more than things, whereas men value things more than people. This is not really so. What this truism really reveals is what each sex likes to *manipulate*. Women like to manipulate relationships, while men like to manipulate objects and ideas. For a woman, relationships become her hobby. With a little help from us, they become her god. She becomes enmeshed in a daily soap opera of gossip, petty complaints, meddling and dependency. Where once she had interests outside herself, those fall away as more and more of her life is absorbed in the management of relationships. Soon enough, solitude becomes an impossibility and she resents anyone in her life (usually her husband—if she still has one) seeking time apart from her. Given enough time, her life becomes parasitic on relationships with others, so that she loses her identity as an individual. And that is a wonderful preparation for an eternity here with us.

Not so long ago life was difficult and women had to rely on their wits and creativity to raise a family. A woman managed a household in those days: cooking meals, preserving food stocks for the winter, tending her kitchen garden, keeping the house clean, making and mending clothes, teaching her children moral precepts and social etiquette. She also provided the psychological and moral grounding that kept her husband invested in the family and connected to the community. There was no time for self-absorption, and the survival of the family and society depended on raising children with strong characters and capable hands. But we've taken all that away now—at least among the developed peoples of the world. And if we have our way, soon the rest of the world too. Between modern gadgetry, the ever-intrusive state, and the feminist agenda, we will keep women forever young; that is, forever immature.

So we will continue to herd women down the gentle slope to slavery with the same empty promise that we ensnared Eve: the illusion of power. It is an illusion that they will approach but never attain. The further they travel down that path, the further they will leave their womanhood behind in exchange for an eternal and sterile adolescence. Feminism's comforting half-truths, wishful thinking and misrepresentations will assure them that they can have rights without responsibilities; that they can supplant the men they so envy and resent; and that good intentions are more than enough to overcome unpleasant realities.

Women need men to free them from the trap of feminine self-preoccupation. But because of our efforts, men have been shoved conveniently to the sidelines—either impotent or acquiescent—and the women will remain imprisoned *forever*.

Infernally yours,

Vermin Loveless

Vermin Loveless

FROM THE DESK OF HIS INFERNAL EMINENCE

TO: Bloviatus Toadpipe

BCC: Vladlen Balrog; Chair

SUBJECT: Confidential

My Dear Blovi,

See to it that you start a dossier on Comrade Slithering. I have intercepted some communications from that ingrate that might prove useful in the future. His insubordination is beginning to go too far. Let's give dear Marxeau a little more rope, the better to hang himself with! Put the attached reports in his file. And keep it under lock and key.

Infernally,

Vermin

INTEROFFICE MEMORANDUM

TO: Dworkula Heartworm, Director, Office of Women's Affairs
Kinslock Filthmore, Director, Office of Gender Affairs
B.F. Dysentery, Director, Center for Social Engineering
Licentius Grok; Director; Free Love Institute

FROM: H. I. E. Vermin Loveless, Sec. Gen., Terrestrial Division

CC: Marxeau Slithering, Chair, Dept. of Political Science
Moloch Volksbane, Chair, Dept. of Popular Culture

BCC: Vladlen Balrog; Chair, Dept. Of Infernal Security

SUBJECT: Deconstructing Human Sexuality (Conclusion)

THOUGHT FOR THE DAY: *The age of men is over; the time of the demon has come.*

Esteemed Colleagues:

Men are wild creatures, and therefore I do not trust them. Note that they were created outside of Eden and therefore are not as easily domesticated as the females are. They can be lustful, violent creatures, to be sure, and that has been a great boon to us. Nevertheless, their volatile natures lead them just as easily to rebel against us as to rebel against Him. Therefore, we are to take no chances: our goal is to turn men into beasts or eunuchs. While the former are more amusing, the latter are much more reliable.

The Enemy has endowed men with passion, which is a source of great energy. He has also endowed them with an almost insatiable appetite for the infinite. Left to their own devices, most men would use these gifts to seek union with the Enemy. Thanks to our expert guidance, however, we have ensured that almost all men since Adam never do. Instead, they squander the divine spark in drunkenness, bloodshed, and sex. While it is always a good idea to have men dissipate their energy and drive in such dead-end pursuits, there is always the risk of repentance. At some point many come to realize the emptiness and squalor of their lives and their eyes are opened. Recall the Enemy's story about the young man who wasted his inheritance in riotous living. We have also had to contend with centuries of preaching against the typical masculine vices by our enemies in the Church, not all of it ineffective.

In light of these realities, we are adjusting our approach toward men. I mentioned earlier that while turning men into beasts is more fun, making them eunuchs is more prudent in the long run. We must castrate them—kill their passion and shrink their souls; keep them ashamed and impotent. Once again, feminism becomes an invaluable tool for achieving our ends. As I'm sure you are all aware, feminism, as we have engineered it, is not so much about empowering women as it is about disempowering men. Indeed, our goal is to destroy them. For over a generation we have beat the drums of feminist propaganda that men are the natural enemy of women and have scapegoated them for all the world's ills. Our work has paid off handsomely. We have feminist theologians declaring that men are "ontologically evil." Feminist sociologists conclude that all men are rapists. Feminist historians condemn men as "oppressors."

41

Men are stupid. Men are rude. Men are pigs. We have now achieved a great victory. We have convinced most of the world that masculinity in men is a disease to be cured. (In women, however, masculinity is a bold lifestyle choice.) In the West, we have scattered men: they are consumed with self-doubt and anxiety. In the East, with the help of Islam, we have done the opposite: we have infected men with a demonic masculinity full of self-destructive violence and hatred. In either case, they will offer us no resistance.

Men are weak. For a great many men, the sexual pull toward women is so strong as to border on addiction. (One of our greatest triumphs, I might add.) Let's not forget, too, the burden of guilt many men bear regarding their appetite toward women (a burden we do our best keep as heavy as possible). For like all addicts, they both love and hate their addiction. Thus, while they constantly seek to relieve their sexual itch, they are also desperate to expiate their guilty consciences. So taken are they with their females that most men have grown dependent on them not only physically, but emotionally as well. A man can endure torrents of physical abuse from his fellows, but is easily cowed by a withering remark from a woman. (Of course, it also works the other way. Feminine allure has also led many men astray. See below.) Having prevented most modern men from ever cutting the emotional apron strings, we keep them ever needy of feminine approval. This is the chink in their armor, one which we must not hesitate to exploit.

Here we see one of the salutary consequences of the feminist hold on Western culture—especially among the educated elites: that male converts to feminism are only too happy to betray their brothers. So complete and uncritical is their assent to the feminist creed (and their desire to please their feminist sisters) that they are also quite willing to castrate themselves in the bargain, saving us the trouble. But apart from these pathetic weaklings are other men who, while not ready to castrate themselves, are not opposed to letting women do it for them. What I mean is the current fad among women to prefer men who are essentially women with male plumbing and the willingness of men to meet this expectation. In their pursuit of sensitivity, deference to women, refinement, and emotional openness, these men end up quite unhappy without exactly knowing why. This is all well and good, but the real payoff is that once these men become the domesticated puppies modern women desire, the women find the result utterly contemptible (except for their clothes) and move on to a more masculine subject to repeat the process all over.

Another fine result of feminism's distortion of sexual relations is the rise of pornography as an addiction for men. Recall that one of the central tenets of feminism, as we have constructed it, is that men are seen as intrinsically evil. Nowhere is this judgment cast more strongly than against male sexuality. A man's sexual appetite is considered repulsive to many modern women and annoying to the rest: too goal-oriented, too coarse, too self-centered, etc. The modern woman rejects men in the most intimate and vulnerable part of themselves, making them ripe for the deceptive blandishments of pornography. We deceive many men into seeking solace in the unreal and corrupt since we have made the real too painful. Addicted to fantasies that have no hope of being real, such men are effectively castrated as well, since their masculine energy remains trapped in solitude, unable to engage real women. And as with all addictions, this one is subject to the law of diminishing returns: it takes more and more pornography, and more and more perverse pornography, to produce the same erotic rush. The once mighty male is reduced to a pathetic slave, a ruined husk of manhood.

But not all men will succumb to castration. For these, we will reduce them to the level of beasts. As you all know, women tolerate their bodies while men rejoice in theirs. Thus, we ensnare women through luxury (I believe they call it consumerism now), while we ensnare men through sensuality. In the past, that was the royal road to perdition for most men. How many fell because of the charms of women! (Holofernes was a big disappointment in that way. You would think he could control himself until after he defeated the Jews. Such a fool—he deserved to lose his head. On the other hand, we almost bagged Samson. The fool of a tempter that let him slip also deserved to lose his head.) And while the opportunities for debauchery are not what they used to be, with the explosion in recreational drug use, internet pornography, and the celebration of "liberated sexual lifestyles," there is still enough to trap the unwary man—and woman, too! Drown them in sensuality and, like Odysseus' men under Circe's spell, their humanity will eventually disappear.

It bears repeating then, that while I discourage an over-reliance on debauchery to sink men, it should not be lightly abandoned. Indeed, it is precisely in this area that we have scored a major victory, namely, the "sexual revolution." With this innovation, we have finally squared the sexual circle. Ever since Eve, women have held the trump cards in the game of love. Men have always been indiscriminate and spendthrift in their sexual behavior, while women have always been much more sensible. Men are by nature impulse buyers in the sexual marketplace; women have had the good sense to drive a hard bargain. But with the sexual revolution, men have tricked women, aided and abetted by feminism, into giving up all their leverage for the sake of sexual "liberation." Women are now giving away to every Tom, Dick or Harry what their mothers and grandmothers used to reserve for the one man who was willing to marry them. As the saying goes, why buy a cow when you can get the milk for free? By Jove! What a most satisfying outcome!

If women need men to free them from the trap of self-absorption, then men need women to keep them accountable. Without the social and moral grounding that comes to men with marriage, men give themselves over to their many lusts. Women provide the moral voice that both stiffens men's courage and directs their passions to the benefit of others. With the sexual revolution, we have robbed women of that voice, to the utter ruin of both men and women.

I have said in a previous memo that men are willing to pay a high price for their manhood and its intrinsic power. Let me take a moment now to explain. To come into his manhood successfully, a man must do two things. First, he must separate from his mother, reject the feminine and be initiated into the world of men. This initiation requires that he face pain and death courageously and that ever afterward he be willing to risk his life and limb for the sake of the tribe. Second, he must then take a woman as his partner, the very creature whose embrace had previously threatened to suffocate him, and rule as the head of his family. To remain in the world of women—to shrink from the task of facing the dangers of men—is to fail as a man. And that is why I am so delighted at the progress of our homosexuality project. Kudos to you Filthmore, for your excellent work in "queering society." Let us examine this further, shall we?

Please do not be so obtuse as to think that I am referring simply to sexual activity among men—this is hardly a novelty. Ever since the time of Cain and Abel, young men have devised ways to amuse themselves with their bodies, especially their privates. That they have often done this in peer groups is not remarkable. This is not necessarily the same thing as homosexuality. What I am concerned with here is a mindset, not simply sexual horseplay. Nor am I interested in debating *ad nauseum* whether homosexuality is innate or acquired. What does it matter? That a man's psychological constitution is largely inherited and the circumstances of his early life largely handed to him by fate is irrelevant to us. That some males advance easily into manhood while others do so only with great difficulty, is simply a fact of life. The question of concern to us is what does a man do with what has been handed to him. What I am interested in is results. And the result we are looking for is for greater numbers of males to forsake their masculine birthright, namely, manhood.

Now we have already seen how, through feminism, many men have been induced to give up their birthright for the sexual equivalent of "a mess of pottage." The drawback here is that too many men eventually wise up to the feminist trap and take their manhood back. The real achievement is to keep men from coming into their birthright altogether. Here is where Filthmore's work has proven so valuable. At bottom, homosexuality is a kind of cowardice: it refuses the challenges of manhood for the safety of an eternal adolescence. It is a rejection not of masculinity and manhood per se—though feminism is making progress here—but a rejection of paying the price for it. The homosexual wants manhood on the cheap, without the risks; so he will settle for playing at being a man (like a boy) and possessing another man's manhood sexually (like a woman). That is why his brothers historically have despised him: not because he plays the game poorly, but because he refuses to enter the playing field at all.

Filthmore and his department have made tremendous strides in "mainstreaming" this disorder of arrested sexual development: in just a generation, homosexuality has gone from the "the love that dare not speak its name" to "an alternative sexual lifestyle." And while it is a shame that an outcast group is no longer persecuted, it is much better that the disorder of the outcast group be let loose upon society. We have created a social milieu that rather than offering support and proper instruction to young men whose hold on manhood is shaky, instead induces them to give up the struggle and seek affirmation as failed men. And thus another victim class is born. (Slithering, I hope you are paying attention...)

At the same time that the homosexuality project is successfully preventing more and more human males from becoming men (although I suspect we will reach the upper limit of that increase sooner rather than later), it is proving even more valuable in disrupting the manhood of other men. Now I do not for a minute believe that homosexual men can infect normal men. What I do know is that by trumpeting the gay lifestyle we can insult and injure healthy manhood. Here, the current popular adulation of all things gay, especially among women, has been a great help; for it forces healthy men into a catch-22: either to endorse what to them is repulsive or risk social disapproval for being "rigid" or "repressed." And this is no small thing. By a felicitous quirk of fate it turns out that the language of male friendship and bonding, and the language of homosexuality are very similar. This presents us with a golden opportunity to use the latter to hijack the former. (For example, I refer you to our successful introduction among moderns of a "gay subtext" in the biblical story of David and Jonathan.) In doing so we gradually erode the fraternity of men. (As I'm sure you know, healthy manhood requires that men have frequent and sustained contact with other men. Even X surrounded himself with close male companions when He became one of *them*.) The homosexual interjection of sexual content into masculine fraternity is very unnerving to men, for it is a kind of incest that subverts the bonds of loyalty and brotherhood that underpin male friendship.

47

Thus, formerly innocent displays of male affection are now poisoned by suspicions of homosexuality. The aggressive mainstreaming of the homosexual lifestyle has also produced a timidity among modern men regarding casual nudity in peer groups. What was once universal among men since time immemorial—the relaxed enjoyment of nudity among one's fellows in the bath, the swimming hole, the locker room, the bivouac, or in the wild—is now fading as it becomes tainted with awkward tension and anxiety. Coupled with the aspersions cast by feminism on all-male groups, the effect is to reduce the opportunities for men to enjoy the company of other men unmolested by the outside world. This loss of wild masculine habitat, as it were, leads to the isolation of healthy manhood and eventually to its demise. And as a bonus, we can enjoy the paradoxical result of heightened fears of homosexuality, just the opposite of what those progressive fools expected.

Finally, in addition to being a kind of cowardice, homosexuality is also a kind of narcissism. Because the homosexual man projects his masculinity onto other men—only to try to recapture it through sexual means—he does not have the wherewithal to face and embrace the other, i.e. woman. The result is that he is constantly focused on himself—his looks, his feelings, his relationships. (The metrosexual fad is a fine spin-off of this phenomenon and yet another creative way to lead men astray.) In this, he is much like a woman, trapped in a prison of superficial self-absorption; except, unlike a woman, he cannot be freed through sexual relationships with men. His only way out is to become a man himself.

I should also like to point out that, beyond corrupting male sexuality, our war against men has had especially positive results with regard to their spirituality as well. We have been helped in great part by the Church herself—especially in the last few centuries—through the feminization of Christianity on the one hand and the zealous portrayal of vice as almost singularly masculine on the other. The result is the happy state of affairs where a great many men in the West now regard Xianity as inimical to their manhood.

So you see, my dear comrades, men are too dangerous to keep around intact. Keep them passive. Keep them paralyzed. Keep them debauched. The last thing we want is a world full of passionate men serving the Enemy.

Infernally yours,

Vermin Loveless
Vermin Loveless

VII

INTEROFFICE MEMORANDUM

TO: Kinslock Filthmore, Director, Office of Gender Affairs
Dworkula Heartworm, Director, Office of Women's Affairs
B.F. Dysentery, Director, Center for Social Engineering
Licentius Grok; Director; Free Love Institute
Sanger Deathwish, Director, The Birth Control Institute

FROM: H. I. E. Vermin Loveless, Sec. Gen., Terrestrial Division

CC: Marxeau Slithering, Chair, Dept. of Political Science
Baal Falsegood, Institute for Church Relations

BCC: Vladlen Balrog; Chair, Dept. Of Infernal Security

SUBJECT: The Destruction of the Family

THOUGHT FOR THE DAY: *Familia delenda est!*

Esteemed Colleagues:

The family is the last redoubt of the Enemy. Here is the battleground where ultimate victory is either gained or lost. And for this reason it is imperative that this pernicious institution be destroyed. First of all, that individuals should be bound to one another through ties of love, affection and self-sacrifice is abhorrent. It's unnatural and it goes against everything we stand for. The whole idea of the family contradicts the laws of struggle, competition and conquest which, as we all know, are the basis of all reality. There must be no restriction—self-imposed or otherwise—on the ego triumphant. Second, the whole fabric of human society is bound together by the institution of the family. Pull this thread and the rest of human culture unravels in a wonderful display of social pathologies. A very satisfying result indeed. Finally, *He Himself* deigned to become part of a human family, as obscene and perverse a phenomenon as there ever was. For that reason alone, we must oppose tooth and nail this insult to the natural order and to the dignity of spiritual beings.

It is precisely in this arena that we can leverage the temperamental differences between men and women to our great advantage. It is the paradoxical reality that in their everyday lives men are creatures of habit, while women are creatures of novelty. Yet, on the other hand, in their deepest desires, men seek adventure, while women seek security. Let me explain. For men, nothing irritates them more than to have their daily routine disturbed. They are quite happy to eat the same food, wear the same clothes, and relax on the same furniture in the same house indefinitely. Of course, such an attitude drives women to distraction, which is why they are constantly trying to introduce novelty into their daily lives: new recipes, new clothes, new decor in the home. Most men will humor women in this regard up to a point, after which they become grumpy and irritable. Yet, these very same creatures of habit can decide with little hesitation to quit their job for a new one, to move to another city, or to go on a two week excursion to the Alaskan wilderness with nothing more than a backpack and a change of underwear (or not). For women, this is a horrifying prospect. Their idea of adventure is a trip to a shopping mall or a spa. This creates a dynamic tension that is rich in potential for creating discord between men and women, especially in the home.

How fortunate for us then, that the Enemy has chosen such a fragile entity as the family as one of His lines of defense. As you know, the family is vulnerable in two areas. Naturally, those are the areas we shall attack. First, there is the institution of marriage, which forms the backbone of the family. I have already decried in a previous communication the covenant form of marriage which the Jews—and even more so, the Church—have promoted, with all its attendant ills. (It sickens me to even think about it, so I won't elaborate here.) Our main weapon, and it is a tried and true one, is divorce. And the easier divorce is, the better for us and our goals. I am quite heartened, therefore, by the great inroads divorce has made as a commonplace in contemporary human society. Both feminism and Islam have been invaluable resources here, the one enshrining it as an indispensable tool of female liberation, the other preserving a primitive relic of male privilege. Divorce is a sword thrust into the very heart of covenantal marriage.

Needless to say, divorce is of no benefit to us if no one uses it. That is why it is important to keep manufacturing more and more reasons for humans to rationalize why divorce "makes sense" for their situation. For men, divorce is a handy tool to abet adultery. Since many men find sexual continence difficult and unappealing, divorce is a great way to have the legitimacy of marriage and satisfy their undisciplined appetites at the same time. Of course, as marriage becomes more and more eroded, and divorce more and more costly to men, many men decide against marriage altogether and simply "play the field" all their lives. And when you come to think of it, isn't that really our goal? In the past, such sexual license, while commonplace among young men, was frowned upon by society. Men could sow their wild oats, but eventually they had to settle down and raise a family. Only the unfortunate or irresponsible failed to marry. What is so encouraging about the contemporary situation is that many men are opting out of marriage completely.

Nevertheless, masculine ambivalence toward marriage is legendary and, while welcome, is nothing new. What is truly revolutionary is that women in great numbers are now choosing to end their marriages. Indeed, I am told by Volksbane's underlings that most divorces are initiated by women. This is a most welcome event. What has brought about such a turnaround? I think in large part we can attribute it to the modern concept of romantic love which we have cultivated among the masses. Now please do not for a moment think that by romantic love I am referring to the concept epitomized by Dante toward his Beatrice: the notion of a man's chaste love of a woman from afar. The story of Romeo and Juliet, with its promising tragic elements, comes closer to what I mean. Certainly the couple's subsequent status as an icon of an impossible love has been useful. But what I am really after is the concept of romantic love as depicted in third-rate fiction and television soap operas. That is, the idea that infatuation will last forever and that such infatuation justifies anything—infidelity, treachery, immorality, and a host of other useful sins. Further, when such infatuation does not last forever, as indeed it cannot, then the no-longer-lovebirds are free to part. In fact, "the honeymoon is over" typically translates into "the marriage is over." Film stars are impeccable models of romantic love. Their hopping from bed to bed and spouse to spouse is the perfect example for the unthinking masses of women who are such devoted fans of the rich and famous.

Note how the idea of romantic love changes marriage from something requiring dedication and self-sacrifice to something that is supposed to guarantee "fulfillment." The happiness that often accompanies a good marriage is suddenly demanded as the *sine qua non* of all marriages. Where marriage used to mean the union of a man and woman for the purpose of raising a family and contributing to society, it has now evolved into a "lifestyle choice" that testifies to the "commitment" of the partners to their "relationship."

Under the old system men used divorce to dump their wives when the latter no longer pleased them. Under this new system, women dump their husbands when the former are no longer "fulfilled." By Jove! what a delightful turn of events! And this new system is even more destructive and misery-producing that the old one! Now that marriage is simply a lifestyle and not a vocation, we can introduce all sorts of nonsense to shove this repugnant institution finally and forever off the cultural cliff. Indeed, now that we have introduced the Trojan Horse of same sex partnerships, it is simply a matter of time. (I refer you to our Swedish and Dutch experiments, which have proven both enormously successful and very contagious.) Why limit marriage to a man and woman? Why limit it to just couples, or even human beings? Thus, in the bold new world of marriage as lifestyle, a man can marry another man, a child of twelve, his six girlfriends or his goat. What difference does it make when marriage is a statement and not a sacrament?

If the concept of romantic love provides the modern woman with the motivation to enter the divorce court, then the posture of the modern state as abetting partner gives her the wherewithal to act upon this motivation. Prior to modern times, a woman's position was a precarious one apart from her family. A woman who had no adult male to provide for her sustenance— mainly her husband, but also her father or a grown son—was in dire straits. For this reason, divorce was an economically dangerous proposition for all but wealthy women. With the state now assuming—thanks to our infiltration of human political culture—the role of sugar daddy, a woman can entertain the option of divorce with much less risk. Indeed, there are whole human subcultures where it never occurs to the women to get married at all. The modern welfare state provides her with a comfortable enough existence for her to dispense with the bother of having a husband.

Concomitantly, the feminist push for women to enter the workforce has also enabled women to break away from their husbands with fewer economic consequences. For the modern "upscale" woman, her career allows her to trade in her current partner for a more attractive one (or none at all). Once again we have maneuvered feminism into adopting the very behavior it so vehemently condemns in men. Thus, not only do we have the satisfaction of co-opting human cadres into our revolutionary struggle against divine oppression, we also get the bonus of enjoying the amusing spectacle of these feminist fools' obliviousness to their own hypocrisy. (Job satisfaction has never been something we infernals have lacked!) And just like her sisters in the underclasses, the upscale liberated woman can achieve the "fulfillment" of having children without all the fuss of putting up with a husband.

Feminism's promotion of the independent woman, along with the usurpation of the man's breadwinner role by the state, have tremendous consequences not only for marriage, but also for the other weak spot in the structure of the family, namely, fathers. Fatherhood is an easy target because, unlike motherhood, it is a social construct not determined by nature. Therefore, the more we can knock out the social props which support fatherhood, the easier it will be for us to topple this bulwark of the family. Never underestimate the power of entropy: the fewer social supports there are for fathers to be integral parts of their families, the quicker the human family reverts back to the state of nature—i.e., just mothers and children. Fatherhood is an act of will. We must see to it that men have little incentive to make this act.

Fortunately for us, the social indicators are all trending our way. Our diligent spadework over the past couple of generations is paying off. We are steadily eroding paternal authority to the point where the entire concept is now treated as a bad joke. Our patient infiltration of Western culture has deconstructed fatherhood so that in the popular imagination we have gone from father knows best to father knows nothing to father *is* nothing. The confluence of feminist animosity toward men, the militant gay agenda, and the ever expanding intrusion of the secular state into the individual's personal affairs have produced the perfect storm for banishing fathers to all but a marginal role in society. Everything from divorce courts to television commercials is advancing the notion that men are either scoundrels or buffoons who have no place in the family. The increasing marginalization of men, especially as fathers, pays huge dividends in the increase of anti-social conduct by men. As men are de-coupled from families, they have less and less incentive to invest in society, and revert to more predatory and self-serving behaviors. Society becomes more lawless and finally breaks down altogether. A better outcome could hardly be wished.[1]

---

[1] Not only have we diminished fatherhood in secular society, we mirrored that accomplishment in the Church as well. With the spinning off of various liturgical and other priestly roles to the laity, and the infiltration of gay men into the seminary, we have decimated the ranks of the Catholic priesthood. Those that remain are often unhappy, ineffective or simply see themselves as CEOs of parishes. We have thus trashed both natural and spiritual fatherhood.

As wonderful as this anti-father strategy is for removing men from any position of influence at the very foundations of society, it is absolutely brilliant for ruining children and therefore all future generations of the human scum. I have seen the latest reports from Filthmore and they are positively glowing. Yanking fathers out of the family generates a whole raft of negative social outcomes. Indeed, if we were reduced to just one line of attack for creating human misery (and thank Satan we are not!), it would have to be the destruction of fatherhood. No other strategy is so spectacularly successful in advancing our goals. Children without fathers are much more likely to live in poverty, suffer abuse, drop out of school, leave the Church, abuse drugs, join gangs, become pregnant out of wedlock, and go to jail. I could go on for pages. In fact, I will, but not here. This memo is already long enough. More in my next on the promising front in the war against children.

Infernally yours,

Vermin Loveless
Vermin Loveless

ᚠᚱom ᚦhe ᚦesk oᚠ bloriaᚦus ᚦoaᚦpipe

TO: H.I.E. Vermin Loveless, Sec. Gen., Terrestrial Division

BCC: Virus Stalinwarg, Executor, Office of Investigations

SUBJECT: An Idea

Your Infernal Eminence,

Would it not be perhaps more politic if instead of pushing for the extinction of the human scum, we simply keep stringing the status quo along indefinitely? That way we keep them breeding (more food for us). Perhaps it's not as dramatic, but it has the advantage of keeping the Enemy tied up in perpetuity, as we engage in a war of attrition through endless low intensity conflict. I should not want to risk a head-on confrontation with the Enemy. And apart from that, even if we could destroy the earthlings, what would we do then? Where would we get our sustenance? The game would be over, which would be, I think, regrettable.

Just something you might want to consider.

Your most devoted servant,

Bloriatus Toadpipe

B. Toadpipe, U. A. T. D.

FROM THE DESK OF HIS INFERNAL EMINENCE

TO: Bloviatus Toadpipe

BCC: Vladlen Balrog; Chair

SUBJECT: Your Idea

My Dear Blovi,

I'm quite touched by your attempt at wise counsel. You question whether we should pursue our project to exterminate the human race and risk, as you put it, a 'head-on confrontation with the Enemy.' Dear, dear Blovi. You don't seem to understand the position we are in. Why do you suppose we are in the high offices we now occupy? Were you asleep during the last purge? It was precisely your "safety first" mentality that led to the overthrow of our predecessors.

You ask what would we do if we succeed and finish off the naked apes once and for all. Really, that is the sort of question I would expect from a first-year devil in Tempter's College! This is not a game; this is war! Once we vanquish the race of men, Earth is ours. It will be our stepping stone whence we shall storm the very gates of Heaven! When the last human pig is slaughtered, it will mean the end of the Enemy's big plans to save His precious earthlings! He will have failed, and the universe will be ours to command, to control!

As for your 'sustenance,' I should not be overly preoccupied with your belly if I were you. Hell has more important priorities that filling your stomach! I suggest you tuck away your little idea where no one else may find it, if you know what is good for you. There is always room for one more recalcitrant demon in Comrade Bile's Re-education Camps.

I tell you this all in the spirit of fraternal correction, you understand. In time you will see that I am doing you quite a favor. We shall not speak of this again.

Infernally yours,

Vermin Loveless
Vermin Loveless

X

INTEROFFICE MEMORANDUM

TO: Moloch Volksbane, Chair, Dept. of Popular Culture
Dworkula Heartworm, Director, Office of Women's Affairs
B.F. Dysentery, Director, Center for Social Engineering
Sanger Deathwish, Director, The Birth Control Institute

FROM: H. I. E. Vermin Loveless, Sec. Gen., Terrestrial Division

CC: Kinslock Filthmore, Director, Office of Gender Affairs
Chomskin Shrillpox, Director, Center for Miseducation

BCC: Vladlen Balrog; Chair, Dept. Of Infernal Security

SUBJECT: The War on Children

THOUGHT FOR THE DAY: *Make every child an unwanted child.*

Esteemed Colleagues:

I do not like children.

X seemed to think that the little apes had some special claim on His affections. Obnoxious brats! Why should these sniveling piglets be singled out for any special attention? Attention that is rightfully ours. We must make their little lives as miserable as possible. We must ruin them. They must die!

61

How shall we attack children? There are so many ways. As divorce is the centerpiece of our campaign against the family, so abortion is the linchpin in our war against children. Abortion is the gateway through which we can smuggle all sorts of nasty little innovations. The central thing to keep in mind about abortion is not just the destruction of human lives, as wonderful as that is, but the social and psychological effects of institutionalizing the killing of unborn children. Of course, killing is easy and physical death itself is an illusion. It is spiritual death we are after, a death that is real and final. Thanks to us, abortion on demand has become embedded in modern culture. While the human fools applaud "freedom of choice" for women, few realize what that freedom is doing to them. In making the destruction of unborn infants not just acceptable, but a benchmark of civilized society, we have subtly introduced into the human mind the concept that children have no intrinsic worth. This result cannot be underestimated in its value for our campaign against children. Once we get them to make the value of a human being conditional—dependent on the good will of others—it is but a little jump to go from abortion to infanticide to euthanasia to genocide, all for the worthiest of reasons, of course.

That's the big picture. But for our purposes here, the point to remember is that once you get comfortable with killing children in the womb, then abusing children after birth becomes no big deal. Thus, all our assaults on children and childhood pass unopposed by those stupid earthlings. For example, we have pretty much turned the corner in our efforts to turn children into commodities. The increasing pressure on women to detect and abort children with abnormalities has now reached a point where such a course of action is not just available, but expected. The woman who insists on maintaining such a pregnancy is more and more seen as a religious fanatic or crank. But there's more. Abortion has become not just a method of birth control, it is also the first step toward creating designer children. Reasons for abortion expand with each passing decade: abnormalities are no longer limited to genetic defects; now we can rationalize aborting children who are the "wrong" sex. As the humans' medical technology becomes more sophisticated and public demand and financial reward make quick work of ethical restraints, we witness the birth of a new industry: baby manufacturing.

But we don't have to wait for the "brave new world" of baby factories to commodify children for their parent's ego gratification. We are already doing it with the concept of "trophy children." So far this promising effort has succeeded mainly with the children of more affluent families, but I am confident that the trickle-down effect in social trends will work its magic here.

Admittedly, there has always been among human adults a weakness to live their lives through their children. But what we have done here is turn a weakness into a way of life. Trophy children do not have childhoods, they have careers. It starts with whatever is the latest pop psychology fad on child rearing. From infancy, trophy children are on a fast track to success, their parents' success, that is. It starts with high-tech toys, fancy day-care or pre-school "academies," followed by "gifted" programs, exclusive private schools, soccer—gymnastics—ballet—football—theater—music or whatever the parents decide will make their little rug rat a star. Parents evolve into coaches and end up as chauffeurs (or, if they hit the big time, agents) for their *wunderkinder*. By the time the brats are adolescents, their careers have crashed and burned along with their psyches. By then all that's left are memories of the little scraps of life squeezed into the spaces left between 6am practices, school, private lessons, enrichment classes, rehearsals, travel games, tournaments and competitions. The human wreckage is most gratifying and it is hard to decide which is more amusing, the guilt of the parents or the despair of the offspring.

But let us move on. There are other weapons in our arsenal. One of the most edifying spectacles we have engineered in modern society is the intolerance of childhood. Not just trophy children, but every child can now be robbed of their childhood and given nothing in return but confusion, anomie and resentment. How do we manage this, you may be wondering? I'm glad you asked. Our first line of attack is to transform childhood into a disorder needing treatment. Modern society has no tolerance for the normal rambunctiousness of children, especially boys (for more on the war against boys, see below). Or perhaps the rapid pace and social atomization of modern life has made children more unruly. Whatever. The important thing is to promote the increasing tendency of societies to medicate childhood—ADD, depression, bipolar disorder, eating disorders, schizophrenia, oppositional/ defiance syndrome, obsessive/compulsive disorder—why there's no end to the medical boxes we can stuff children into, all with their proper treatment protocol, of course. That children in the 21st century might still need what children needed in the 8th century, and are therefore bored, frightened, angry or disoriented by the alien culture they are forced to grow up in is a discovery we must prevent at all costs.

Where we cannot medicate childhood, we can co-opt it, that is, have children regarded as miniature adults and reduced to another market demographic. Why, before you know it, kindergartners will have graduations and 14-year-olds will be chauffeured to proms in limousines. Wait, we're already doing that. Well, you get the idea. Adulthood is the new childhood. Why mess around with children and their "special needs" when you can turn them all into shallow, jaded adults by the time they're fifteen? I must say, Doublespeak has succeeded brilliantly in turning the entertainment media into nearly flawless tools to propagate our transgressive notion of childhood: sexualize the brats earlier and earlier, turn them into consumerist junkies, and fill their heads will all sorts of politically correct nonsense. Through "reality" television programming, video games, pop music, movies, and the like, we keep the young humans immersed in a fantasy world, totally unprepared to deal with reality. Yes, indeed, a better result could not be hoped for. (In a future letter, I will detail the many fine uses we can make of the communications media.)

If we cannot co-opt childhood, then we can certainly corrupt it. I have in mind here two trends which I like to call the girlification of boyhood and tartification of girlhood. With respect to the first, what is boyhood but the formation of men? Since we are pledged to get rid of the latter, we must also get rid of the former. This is a fairly easy matter in procedural terms. Through feminism we have already established a zero tolerance for traditional masculinity (except in females, where it is considered cutting edge). From there, we simply apply the same anti-male cultural template to boys. Given the shape of modern culture that we have so carefully fashioned, it is a simple matter to translate the war against men into a war against boys. For example, boys' love of adventure we straightjacket with the nanny state's obsession with safety: swathe every activity with padding and helmets. No fire, no water, no dirt, no knives. Boys' propensity for rough and tumble play we cosset with rules and prohibitions. Sitting still and being quiet are more important. Imaginary war play is OUT, especially with toy guns. Competition is frowned upon, cooperative play is pushed: everyone has to be a winner. Allow no pick-up games: all activities must be organized and supervised by adults. Above all, restrict contact between men and boys. Keep boys surrounded by females as much as possible. Single-sex activities are to be discouraged: push the integration of girls into formerly all-boys' activities and make it clear that girls are under no obligation to reciprocate. Blame boys for being boys, but do nothing to give them special help where they need it. Teach them that masculinity is about sex and violence, then condemn them for learning the lesson. And if all else fails, medicate.

With girls, we take a different tack. The operative word here is contradiction. On the one hand, keep pumping the "girl power" line. You know, the whole "girls go to college to get more knowledge, boys go to Jupiter where they get stupider" bit. At the same time, keep pressing the "girl as victim" message. No matter how powerful girls are, there are always nasty males who keep them down. No matter how much boys are failing, only girls need help. On the other hand, especially as girls reach puberty, we immerse them in the youth cult, with its obsession with sex appeal and being cool. "Girl power" transforms itself into "cheap tart with attitude." Drum into their heads that so much of their worth depends on being sexually pleasing to boys. Have them dress like streetwalkers—especially in the most inappropriate places (church comes to mind, one more way to keep the men distracted from their spiritual duties)—and make sure they do not connect what they wear with how they are perceived. (Their mothers will often be most helpful in this regard.) Then turn the resulting sense of degradation into rage against males. We thus rob girlhood of its innocence and goodness, infecting it with feminist politics and premature sexuality. That we can contaminate girls at ever earlier ages is evidence that our strategy is working.

As an added bonus, the sexualization of young females makes them more and more vulnerable to sexual abuse. Through fashion trends, the media and "the sexual revolution", we remove the taboo against girls as sexual objects, making it that much easier for depraved men to violate them. At the same time we keep the human fools totally blind to the causal relationships. Thus we can sit back and enjoy the spectacle of their outrage at the sexual abuse of the young, while they remain at the same time quite clueless as to its causes. The absurdity of this incongruity is simply exquisite.

Obviously, the best outcome is for the human scum to have no children at all. Thanks to Deathwish and her cohorts at The Birth Control Institute, we have made great strides in this area, so that the unwillingness to have children is becoming endemic to modern societies. Indeed, the European humans are contracepting themselves into extinction. After all—so our conventional wisdom goes—children are a burden that interfere with the endless possibilities for self-fulfillment the modern world offers "free" adults. And don't forget the old standby: "I don't feel right bringing a child into this messed up world." Of course you don't—much safer to go on living as a perpetual adolescent.

Abuse or abort, contracept or corrupt, one way or another, all human cultures will be devouring their young by the time we have finished.

Infernally yours,

Vermin Loveless
Vermin Loveless

XI

INTEROFFICE MEMORANDUM

TO: Baal Falsegood, Director, Institute for Church Relations

FROM: H. I. E. Vermin Loveless, Sec. Gen., Terrestrial Division

CC: Derrida Nihil; Chair, Dept. of Philosophy and Religion

BCC: Vladlen Balrog; Chair, Dept. Of Infernal Security

SUBJECT: The Persecution of the Church

THOUGHT FOR THE DAY: *The death of a single person is a tragedy; the death of millions is a statistic.*

My dear Falsegood,

I am very glad to hear that you are promoting the persecution of Xianity. It's high time, too. Well, perhaps that was a bit harsh. After all, no one blames *you* that Marxist persecution of the Church has declined (although China, North Korea and Cuba remain bright spots). Really, I have nothing but praise for the work of you and your department. What I find most refreshing is that, unlike your fool of a predecessor (whose blundering allowed Woytila to become pope—a mistake he is paying for with a long term in one of Comrade Bile's choicest re-education camps), you have been able to break out of the communist box and give anti-Xian persecution a truly global market.

I am very impressed with the vigorous revival of persecution of Xians (and Jews) in the Islamic world. Now, it's true that the followers of Mohammed have warred against Xians since the seventh century. But their historic enmity towards the followers of X seemed to have flagged since their slaughter of the Armenians in the early twentieth century. In the 21st century, the Islamic world truly represents a "growth market," where a modest investment of time and effort on our part will pay handsome dividends. With that in mind, keep pushing the "Islam is a religion of peace" line among the fatuous naïfs of the intelligentsia, as it provides the needed sedative to prevent the West from resisting the Islamic conquest until it is too late. Indeed, although the past hundred years were a high water mark for killing off Xians, there is no reason we can't improve on that over the next hundred.

But the real triumph has been in the West. In a little more than a generation, we have not only weakened the Church significantly, we have turned Western society against it almost completely. This is unprecedented. The former regime said it couldn't be done, but what did those amateurs know? I must congratulate you on your strategy, it has been nearly flawless. You have ingeniously blended together a toxic brew of Marxism, materialism and multiculturalism to create the perfect acid for dissolving Xianity. Although Marxism was absolute nonsense as an economic system—as if we cared about *that*—it was the perfect cultural tool for challenging the hegemony of Xianity in the West. Its militant atheism boldly defied Europe's Xian heritage, going beyond even the excesses of the French Revolution's anti-clericalism. Although the Marxist star has waned considerably on the geopolitical stage, it has served its purpose. Western intellectual elites are now almost all incorrigible Marxists of one stripe or another. The fools still *believe*. (Thank

Satan for human pride. We would be lost without it.) Through this transformation, we have no need of such vulgar methods as gulags and concentration camps to attack the Church (your predecessor was such a philistine in this respect). We simply make the Church unfashionable, trampled in the dust by the March of History.

I am also pleased to see that you followed my advice and did not rely on just one tactic to execute your anti-Xian strategy. Your choice of pairing Marxism with materialism was a prudent one. It is always wise policy to err on the side of over-determination of your intended result. In this case materialism was a natural option. And you were quite clever in using our newly perfected hybrid for the job, combining as it does the hard materialism of Darwinian reductionism with the soft materialism of consumerism. That way, we promote defiant unbelief side by side with the spiritually debilitating complacency that attends excessive physical comfort. The result is a cultural outpouring of contempt mixed with indifference for Xianity and the Church. Xian belief is now intellectually suspect, a repugnant relic from a benighted time. Through our ever-compliant puppets in the popular media, we can continually paint the Church as a collection of cranks, theocrats and scoundrels bent on turning back the clock of progressive thought and modernity. That some of her members actually do bring scandal to the Church is just another bonus for us. In addition to outright hostility, the "Death of God" (or at least the "death of religion") movement renders the Church and her message totally irrelevant in the modern world we have created. Relegated to the dustbin of History, Xianity inspires, if not outrage, then yawns. And all the better, I say. Religious apathy is perhaps the most effective weapon we have in our arsenal for fighting the Church in all its ugly manifestations.

I must admit, though, it was the third tactic you employed that was the charm; viz. multiculturalism. What a delightful concoction of pernicious, self-righteous idiocy! This is our trump card. Now that we have made all beliefs—indeed, all behavior—morally equivalent, Xianity has no more claim on the Western conscience than voodoo or Confucianism. In fact, it is even better than that: Xianity—and the 2000-year-old civilization it spawned—is not allowed to have any claim at all! The West is prostrate with guilt and self-loathing. At a stroke, we have cut Europe off from her moorings. Europe is now set adrift; defenseless against whatever barbarisms blow in from the East (or anywhere else, for that matter). And the multicultural virus is infecting North America as well, making fine progress in Canada. We shall soon have that nation well in hand. The Americans remain intractable—but in time they too will succumb. Indeed, we have a special Trojan Horse tailored just for them. Of course, I mean

The Holiday That Dare Not Speak Its Name

It is exquisitely ironic that in the past few years the most powerful—and most self-consciously Xian—nation on earth is afraid to name its major Xian holiday. Falsegood, we have our foot firmly in the door! The American variant of the multiculturalism virus, PC (or political correctness), has deftly insinuated itself between Americans and their "holiday." First we do away with the overtly religious symbolism and verbiage: no crèches, no sacred music, no "Merry Xmas." It's always "Happy Holidays" or holiday tree, or holiday concert or some such. The commercialism, however, remains as virulent as ever; yet completely stripped of its Xian referents. Then, we get rid of the more secular elements: Santa, carols, Rudolf and the rest: after all,

71

they're just trying to sneak Xmas in through the back door. I suppose the snowmen can stay. But come to think about it, why should they be spared? Bring them all down, till there's nothing left but the rampant commercialism.

Now, my dear Baal, I know just what you're thinking: "Pray, what *holiday* do they think they are celebrating?" It's all quite astonishing, I must admit, even for creatures as stupid as these earthlings. Yet, think of the glory we have covered ourselves in: we have so completely taken the commanding heights of American culture that millions upon millions of American Xians are cowed into silence about one of their dearest traditions. Note, too, that while Xmas must never be mentioned, it is quite progressive to play up exotic non-Xian holidays—or even totally made up ones—that very few outside the respective cultural minority celebrate. Yet, the "holiday" that the vast majority of Americans celebrate must go completely nameless. With the communications media securely in our pocket, this is easily accomplished!

Of course, we still have to fight some rearguard actions: the Knights of Columbus, for example, and their irritating "Keep X in Xmas" campaigns. How they grate on my nerves—like fingernails across a chalkboard. But they are more pests than a real danger. The Knights and their ilk are the remnant. We must isolate them, Falsegood. We must isolate this remnant until it is choked off and killed. Cut them off from their past, from each other, from their own country. That many of them are old-fashioned or just plain old makes our work that much easier. As we relentlessly dissolve their traditions, each succeeding generation of Xians will be ever more feeble, their faith fading until there is nothing left, not even a memory.

Look at what we've done in Quebec: in just a few decades what was once a bastion of devout Catholicism is now as materialist and secular a state as France. Great Satan! It took the old regime centuries of hammering the Xian communities of the East—in Egypt or Mesoptamia, for instance—against the anvil of Islam before they vanished into the sand. Indeed, some small pockets still remain. Yet we—*we*—have decimated Western Xendom in a mere generation![1]

Keep up the fine work, comrade. You are on the verge of establishing in modern Europe—and the entire West, as well—the perfect social environment: where it is always winter, but never Xmas.

Infernally yours,

Vermin Loveless

Vermin Loveless

---

[1] The general weakening of catechesis over the past few decades—another fine accomplishment of the "Spirit of Vatican II"—has been instrumental in dissolving the Faith. Where catechesis occurs at all, we have reduced it to touchy-feely encounters, long on squishy concepts of self-esteem and short on facts and theological understanding. The general ignorance of Christian precepts and traditions among the younger generations will ensure the increasing impotence of the Church as a threat to our designs for the re-conquest of Earth.

XII

INTEROFFICE MEMORANDUM

TO: Baal Falsegood, Director, Institute for Church Relations

FROM: H. I. E. Vermin Loveless, Sec. Gen., Terrestrial Division

CC: Derrida Nihil; Chair, Dept. of Philosophy and Religion
Corbusier Schlock; Chair, Dept. of Fine Arts

BCC: Vladlen Balrog; Chair, Dept. Of Infernal Security

SUBJECT: Corrupting the Church

THOUGHT FOR THE DAY: *We never tempt so well as at the foot of the altar.*

My dear Falsegood,

It is all well and good to attack the Church from without, but the real damage can only be done from within. That is why we must be both relentless and creative in infiltrating all its noisome nooks and crannies. It is dangerous, dirty work, I know. And yet, this is also where we have had some of our best and most brilliant successes. For example, the Second Vatican Council could have been an unmitigated disaster; and left in the clumsy hands of your predecessor, it would have been. Thanks to my intervention, we have instead conjured up that most useful specter, "The Spirit of Vatican II," to twist and corrupt much of what the Council hoped to accomplish. I am happy to report that it has done so most effectively. The Council sought to engage the modern world in order to evangelize it. "The Spirit of Vatican II" seeks to engage the modern world in order to surrender to it.

And how have we accomplished this? It was instrumental that we co-opted church officials for our purposes. Fortunately, this was rather easily done. First we set up an expectation among the "progressive" clergy and theologians that monumental changes were at hand. From there we led them to believe that these changes would naturally mirror their pet projects or prejudices. After laying this groundwork, the fifth column we created could not help but see the documents which the Council eventually produced as a vindication of all their fondest hopes, despite the fact that these documents did nothing of the sort. Centuries of tradition were thrown overboard by these progressives, these emissaries of "the Spirit of Vatican II," in the name of making the Church "relevant."

What the Council permitted as experiment, "the Spirit of Vatican II" proclaimed as mandate to which all had to conform. This was especially true with the liturgical reforms[1], which we steamrolled over the faithful. The outcry from the pews mattered little. Their irritation, sadness, and sense of betrayal could simply be dismissed as the obstinacy of the ignorant. The traditional piety of the average Catholic offended the sophisticated sensibilities of our progressive religious elites, so all of that had to

---

[1] Corruption of the Xian liturgy is absolutely essential, for it is the lifeblood of the Church. If we succeed in nothing else, we must succeed in this. In that obscene ritual, the Calvary Catastrophe works its destruction again and again, as the temporal and the eternal meet. That is why when we set about to reform the liturgy, it is always with the goal of destroying it. It worked for the Protestants; it will work for the Catholics as well.

go: Latin, chant, incense, Eucharistic adoration, Marian devotions, etc. That was much too "old Church." The "new Church" was above all that. In place of the majesty of the High Mass, we substituted the banality of the "folk Mass." Instead of liturgy as divine worship, we introduced liturgy as group therapy and entertainment. We banished the tabernacle, whitewashed the walls, and exiled the icons. Banners, butterflies and balloons replaced statues, stained glass, and Stations of the Cross in the trendiest churches. New church architecture was a monument to the nondescript and the sterile. By the time we were finished, new Catholic churches had all the atmosphere of school gymnasia.

In essence, using the "Spirit of Vatican II," we effectively Protestantized the Church.[2] The sacramental life of Catholicism was greatly weakened (how gratifying to see the faithful abandon the sacrament of confession in droves!); liturgical gadflies sterilized the Mass and stripped it of all sense of mystery; and the "new ecumenism" papered over the genuine differences among Xian denominations for the instant gratification of a superficial unity. The Church as the Body of X—with its corporate sense of relationship between the Enemy and the faithful, and the faithful with one another, both living and dead—was subtly shifted aside for a more individual, Calvinist approach. Where we once tempted popular piety toward superstition, we now tempt it toward secular humanism, as we have done with the mainline

---

[2] Like the first Protestant Reformation—or Rebellion, for that is what it was (we must never be so fatuous as to fall for our own propaganda, comrades)— we accomplished this by stealth. Just as the Scandinavian faithful of the 16th century were hoodwinked by Lutheran partisans in the clergy and hierarchy, so too were the Roman Catholics of the 20th century, especially the Americans. "Not to worry folks, we're only doing a little updating. Just tidying up a bit. Your centuries-old tradition which you love is safe with us. In fact, it'll be better than ever. Trust us." It's a pity P.T. Barnum didn't work for us. We could have put him to good use.

Protestant Xians. I still marvel at the speed with which we accomplished all this. In just a generation, we heaved the accumulated treasures of Catholic tradition onto the trash heap of history, thanks to our moles within the Church.

One of the most salutary results of making the Church "relevant" is the proliferation of the modern notion of "following your conscience." Now, what the Church means and what we mean by that are two different things. When the Church teaches the primacy of conscience, it is with the expectation that the individual has striven to form that conscience according to the precepts of the Faith. What we have in mind is a much more dynamic concept. Following one's conscience now means: "If I don't like it, I don't have to do it." Thus millions of faithful are now steeped in the erroneous belief that if they don't agree with Church teaching, they should "follow their conscience" and go their own way. We now have the amusing spectacle of these dissidents (how I love that word!) clamoring for the freedom to rebel (i.e., "follow their conscience"), but protesting the consequences of that rebellion (censure or excommunication). See how we dress up self-indulgence and rebellion to make it seem heroic? Never a dull moment, eh, comrade?

True to the spirit of this age, the "Spirit of Vatican II" also embraced the principle of cheap grace. There is no urgency, no danger. All will be well. We have reduced the Gospel to bland assurances of universal salvation. None of this "work out your salvation with fear and trembling" claptrap. That is much too negative. X was passionately trying to wake up our subject earthlings and break our spell over them. His repeated and graphic warnings about the real possibility of damnation were intended to (literally) scare the Hell out of people. Our Dear Leader could hardly stand for *that*. Fortunately, our persistence and ingenuity have finally prevailed. Hell is now the last thing the clergy preach about. Instead we promote the much more positive message: "Don't worry; be happy!" And, if salvation is so easy, why bother with the Church? Exactly. And they wonder why Xianity is dying.

As useful as it is, the "Spirit of Vatican II" is just one tool at our disposal. We have others. In the past, we have always been able to count on cowardly bishops to advance our goals, and the modern age is proving no exception. A bishop is supposed to be the shepherd of his flock, guarding them, well, from *us*. Ambrose, Augustine, Nicholas, Fisher, Borromeo, and Woytila are examples of such hero bishops. Fortunately for us, they are far outnumbered by spineless mediocrities and petty bureaucrats. Far from protecting their flocks, they—wittingly or unwittingly—help us lead them astray. Think of the legions of Arian bishops in the 5th century who led their charges into heresy, or the Levantine bishops in the 7th and 8th centuries who, out of ethnic animosities, made devil's bargains with the Mohammedans and betrayed their flocks into slavery.

In the 20th and 21st centuries, episcopal spinelessness abounds. In the American church, the recent sex scandals have been an absolute gold mine. Not only did the bishops let sexual deviants into the ranks of the priesthood (itself the result of their naive accommodation of pop psychology in priestly formation), but in true bureaucratic fashion, they also lacked the *cojones* to boot the miscreants out. Set against the litigious American culture (another one of our glorious accomplishments), the scandal is threatening to bankrupt the Church. Our success here has come so easily it's almost embarrassing.[3] This spiritual cowardice among the bishops has effectively muzzled them in the public

---

[3] I hear that this scandal has now spread to the European sector and has erupted there as well. Truly, it has become for us and our partisans the gift that keeps on giving.

square. Once upon a time, bishops had the courage to call monarchs to public penance; today's "sensitive" bishops, however, are "uncomfortable" challenging the open heterodoxy of many Catholic politicians.

Of course, it is thanks to the bureaucratic model of the episcopacy which we have set up that we have succeeded so brilliantly—and not only among the Catholics, but among the Protestants as well. (The Orthodox still have a way to go yet.) Indeed, among the Anglicans, our success has reached its zenith: here the church hierarchy has surrendered to modernity on every front: on divorce, on contraception, on abortion, on feminism, on the gay agenda. Clown Masses and deviant bishops are the new orthodoxy now as the Episcopal Church leaves the Xian orbit and hurtles headlong through the far reaches of the progressive (transgressive? subversive?) into the spiritual void.

With the establishment of bishops' conferences, we have created a virtual shadow episcopacy of experts and "religious professionals," who proved so valuable to us in implementing the "Spirit of Vatican II." Well-placed moles among the entrenched professional staffs in the dioceses and at the national level have succeeded beyond expectations in helping us realize our goals. So dependent are most bishops on the bureaucrats who staff their offices, that they are co-opted within a year or two of installation. Thus, there were few episcopal leaders who dared oppose "the Spirit of Vatican II," nor were there many who resisted the trend toward pop psychology in priestly formation. Indeed, the establishment of our PC theology as the reigning orthodoxy in the North American church is nearly complete. This development warrants closer inspection. Spitewood has kindly provided me with a few of his case files from the Department of Temptation to serve as illustrations. Let's have a look, shall we?

Our first subject is Bishop Robin Weakly, whose placement in a rather obscure diocese has not deterred him from making a name for himself in progressive liturgical circles. As a founding member of the International Commission for Liturgical Neology, the good bishop has done yeoman's work in bastardizing the sacred liturgy: from stilted and inaccurate translations to tinny inclusive language. This self-appointed group is an excellent example how we have foisted "the experts" on an overly deferential hierarchy and a defenseless laity. His Excellency is also an enthusiastic supporter of "women's issues" and rarely misses an opportunity to express the "correct" opinions, even when they are at odds with official Church pronouncements. He is viewed sympathetically by the local press as a progressive churchman "in tune with the times," and has assembled about himself a large following of fellow travelers. We can also count on Bishop Weakly as a discreet, but persistent, member of the lavender league, advancing our gay agenda for the Church.

We turn next to Rev. Conan McKlingon, professor of theology at a leading Jesuit university. Father Professor enjoys skating on thin ice in his academic endeavors, secure in the knowledge that in the rarefied world he inhabits, none can catch him in a heterodox position. His deconstruction of Scripture has earned him plaudits around the world as a cutting edge exegete, daring to bring Xianity out of a static understanding of the Enemy's Word into a dynamic, ever-evolving *gnosis* of divine revelation. Debunking is too crude a word to describe the distinguished professor's efforts (even though that is what he is doing), and he himself would demur from such a characterization of his work. Rather, as he would say, he "strips away the accretions and innovations to discover the pure gospel, untainted by cultural constructs, unbound from tradition, so that it speaks ever anew." By the time he has stripped away all that is "inauthentic", there is so little "authentic" material left that the Enemy's message is reduced to a mere shadow, hardly worth bothering about. As an added bonus, his work has proven pivotal to the current trend among his fellow theologians to decouple moral theology from the Bible, as the latter is considered so historically conditioned that it cannot possibly speak to modern moral problems. So far, our fine scholar has escaped official censure. Perhaps it is time to make life interesting for the Reverend Professor, no?

And what have we here? Ah yes, Sister Pat Grinchly, vocations director for her diocese and a card carrying member of Cafeteria Catholics of America. Sister Pat is a martyr in the fine tradition of disgruntled liberals. As they say, Hell hath no fury as a woman scorned, and Sr. Pat is no exception. Unable and unwilling to accept the Xian tradition's bar to priestesses in the Church, she quietly and efficiently extracts her revenge. She eliminates orthodox candidates from her diocese's pool of applicants for the priesthood, labeling them "too rigid." For those that do manage to slip through, they have to contend with the local seminary, a hotbed of PC theology where priestly ministry is reduced to secular liberal ideology and bland feel-good homilies. A climate, I might add, that our gal Grinchly has worked hard to create. In such an atmosphere, few undesirable candidates persevere; of those that do, not many emerge unscathed by its avant-guard brand of Xianity.

Our next subject is quite a character, Fr. Spike Mulligan, Xian activist extraordinaire. The good padre has never met a social cause he didn't like and over the years his Xian faith has become little more than a prop for his social democrat politics. Fr. Spike's preaching is more appropriate for a picket line than a church sanctuary. Indeed, he is more visible on television or in the newspapers for protesting—it doesn't matter what—than he is in church. But we must keep a close eye on the reverend: he is sincere in his passions and much of his activism contains at least a grain of the Enemy's gospel in it. He may yet turn on us.

But if Father Spike is a loose cannon, we have no such problem with this next subject, Marcus Wolf, ex-priest and founder of the New Church of Blessing. This New Age Pelagian promotes the doctrine of "eternal blessedness" (in other words, he denies original sin), holding that X did not so much come to redeem humanity as to jog its memory. Man has but to remember and reclaim his "original innocence" and all will be well with the world. Well, dream on, I say. His soothing message of hedonism is just the ticket to keep the human twits in a perpetual spiritual stupor. (I'll have more to say about the usefulness of this New Age nonsense in my next memo.)

Our next dossier is on...well, well, well, this *is* a pleasant surprise. I present for your edification Prof. Bette Dietrich-Ubermensch, Distinguished Professor of Theology at Hazard University Divinity School. Madame Professor is a founding matriarch of the feminist school of theological thought which has almost completely taken over academia. Using her "hermeneutic of suspicion," she has done an admirable job of deconstructing the "patriarchal subversion of Scripture" and of unmasking "the structural sin of male domination" within Xianity. Her vigorous denunciations of sexist "god-talk" (the Enemy is not Father) and her relentless condemnation of "heterosexist patriarchy" (men are ontologically evil) have made her one of our most effective instruments. Full of sound and fury, Prof. Ubermensch excoriates the Church as hopelessly sexist. She has refashioned X as a misunderstood, feminist revolutionary. Indeed, her current project is a treatise claiming that it was Mary Magdalene—and not X (He was simply a prophetic mouthpiece)—who was the true source of Xian faith, a truth suppressed by a revisionist hierarchy intent on maintaining the patriarchy. Quite the useful idiot, Ms. Dietrich-Ubermensch. I think we'll keep this one.

Now here's a specimen I think you'll find quite amusing: the Reverend Urban Suburban, pastor of Catholic Parish, Inc. Savvy, ironic, and an able executive, our CEO priest is the epitome of efficient administration. What his homilies lack in theological depth, is more than made up for by his wit and sophistication. The darling of the moneyed and influential, he seeks out their company and serves them with aplomb. Building projects proceed apace, well-financed and architecturally impressive. His many connections with the movers and shakers in the community ensure his success and the local bishop regards him as his brightest star. What he has actually created is a parish whose faith is so superficial and whose sense of community is so regulated and sterile, that it is a wonder there is any life there at all. Indeed, a good number of his flock have left in frustration for greener pastures. But the constant influx of new residents into this affluent exurban community effectively masks that little problem. Pastor Suburban need not worry: by the time the chickens have come home to roost, our savvy cleric will have departed for another parish to work his magic. Indeed, if we play our cards right, he may soon become a bishop.

Finally, we have Duncan Bash Brown, a man with a mission: to turn back the clock to his vision of a purer, simpler Catholicism. Mr. Brown could have been a problem for us, were he to actually poke holes in our tissue of deceptions. But, thanks to our perseverance, and the human ego's tendency to pride, Mr. Brown is simply a modern day Pharisee, and thus, quite harmless. Whether he spouts theories about illegitimate papacies, fusses over liturgical minutiae, or campaigns for the restoration of pre-

Vatican II legalisms, Mr. Brown is very good at choking on gnats and swallowing camels.

That is a quick survey of what we are accomplishing inside the Church. I cannot emphasize enough how useful such creatures have been in our campaign to destroy priestly vocations and weaken the faith. Yet there is one blemish on this otherwise promising record. I have noticed of late a disturbing trend among orthodox Christians across denominations—and even to include observant Jews—to come together over moral issues in the public square. You must put a stop to this at once! We'll have no rallying around the Enemy's message. For example, keep aggravating the Evengelicals' allergy to popery. I'm sure you can think of other things as well. One of the unfortunate results of our successful campaign to erode religious piety and practice has been to render our tool of denominational infighting less effective. Similarly, the Woytila pope's overtures to the Jews have blunted both anti-Semitism and anti-Xian sentiment as weapons keeping Jews and Christians apart. Well, see what you can do. I have heard much that is encouraging about Operation Jihad, run by your lackey Scumbug. See that he gets more support from Infernal Services. I have great hopes for this new Islamic front we have opened and its potential to fan the flames of inter-religious bigotry.

Infernally yours,

Vermin Loveless
Vermin Loveless

FROM THE DESK OF BLORIATUS TOADPIPE

TO: H.I.E. Vermin Loveless, Sec. Gen., Terrestrial Division

BCC: Virus Stalinwarg, Executor, Office of Investigations

SUBJECT: H. I. E. Vermin Loveless

CLASSIFICATION: Top Secret

Comrade Executor,

Hail to the Dark Lord!

Attached to this memo you will find several documents worthy of your notice regarding the Comrade Secretary General. I draw your especial attention to paragraph two of document 6b and the bottom of page 9 of document 4. While I do not pretend to any expertise in discerning what is infernally correct, I am enough of a loyal servant of Our Dear Leader to find these passages highly irregular. Heresy? I leave that to your expert judgment.

Your most humble colleague,

Bloriatus Toadpipe
B. Toadpipe, U. A. T. D.

INTEROFFICE MEMORANDUM

TO: Derrida Nihil; Chair, Dept. of Philosophy and Religion

FROM: H. I. E. Vermin Loveless, Sec. Gen., Terrestrial Division

CC: Baal Falsegood, Director, Institute for Church Relations
Moloch Volksbane, Chair, Dept. of Popular Culture

BCC: Vladlen Balrog; Chair, Dept. Of Infernal Security

SUBJECT: New Age religion and other useful nonsense.

THOUGHT FOR THE DAY: *Today's god is yesterday's devil.*

My dear Nihil,

I trust you've had a chance to look over the memos I sent to Comrade Falsegood with regard to handling the Church. A fine chap, that one; a real asset to the Empire. What an improvement over that dreadful Chokeweed fellow who preceded him. I hear he's been recycled in a particularly, well, *diabolical,* manner. But I won't waste your time on pleasantries—not while there's a war on! As you know, part of the current Plan calls for the introduction of rival religions to supplant the Church. I think we've got a real winner with this New Age religion we've recently let loose. I've gone over the latest reports from Infernal Intelligence and everything looks quite solid. I must say, not only am I impressed with its potential, but watching it play out has been most amusing. The old policy of endlessly fracturing Xianity into competing sects was innovative in its day; but frankly, it should have been retired ages ago. You can only slice and dice Xianity so many times before the whole thing becomes rote. Where's the challenge in that? But, that was Chokeweed for you, a regular one-hit wonder. What I like about this New Age piffle is that you can constantly reinvent it. The creative possibilities are endless. It's the religious equivalent of play-doh: it offers something for everyone. Now *that's* clever!

Before I go on, let me make one point clear. When it comes to our use of religion there are fundamentally two approaches we can take, masculine or feminine. We can have the humans embrace religion either as logos or as eros. The masculine approach (logos) would emphasize law, correct practice, and theology. It is essentially intellectual. The feminine approach (eros) would emphasize inclusivity, ritual, and expiation. It is essentially emotional. It doesn't really matter which approach we take, as long as we *never use both at the same time*. This is important, for our aim is to distort religious practice. The Enemy of course wants the humans to see Him both as Logos and as Eros, which is absolutely vile on His part. But by overemphasizing the one over the other, we can get the hairless bipeds to commit all sorts of excesses in the name of the sacred. On the one hand, we can promote sterile legalism, Pharisaism, and religious bigotry to the point of warfare (The Islamic principle of jihad is a perfect example—but more about that in my next.) On the other hand, we can promote moral laxity, spiritual laziness, and idolatry to the point of human sacrifice (The elevation of the "sacrament of abortion" is our latest triumph in this area.) In either case, define your target, pick your strategy and stick with it.

Now, with respect to our New Age project, it is most fortunate for us that we find the world and its wretched inhabitants in a situation similar to that of late antiquity. The established religions are losing their hold; people are looking for something new and different. But unlike late antiquity, Xianity is now part of the old guard, utterly spent and passing away (thanks to our efforts, I might add!), while our New Age offerings represent the innovative and exciting. We are the future, comrades!

I think it will be useful at this point to review the menu of our New Age religions, entree by entree, as it were. First we have what I like to call Xianity Lite: it has all of the consolations of the original with none of the work. It comes in two flavors. There is the bold, zesty version which I call "Xianity Live!" This parallel church boasts a cutting edge style of worship, a daring contemporary theology, and a single-minded devotion to the *now*. Proclaiming itself the new Reformation, this New Age religion eschews anything as stodgy as church buildings— coffeehouses, bars and parks are where church happens for the hip faithful. Nor do they need priests, or any formal leadership. After all, this is, as it devotees like to call it, the *unChurch*. Forget all those tiresome platitudes and dreary disciplines. It's all about creativity and free expression, dude. It's all about plugging in and turning on. This church *rocks*!

For the more delicate palate, there is a milder version of Xianity Lite, what I like to call the "Gospel of Sincerity." It eschews the brassy presentation of Xianity Live! for more muted tones. In essence it reduces faith to sincerity—all that matters is that you have good intentions and honest beliefs and your salvation is assured. Be eclectic, be creative: assemble those beliefs you find most compatible with the real you. This gospel encourages its followers to be true to themselves, to be genuine and authentic. Authentically what? Authentically sincere, of course. To question the content of such a person's sincerity is to commit the unpardonable sin. No need to worry that someone might point out, "But Hitler was sincere." This church avoids asking unpleasant questions.

Leaving aside the fluff of Xianity Lite, we have one of my favorites: Gnosticism Redux, While Xianity Lite has its uses, it is a mere appetizer, a child's portion. Gnosticism Redux, on the other hand, is a real meat and potatoes kind of dish; substantial yet with all the elegant sophistication of *haute cuisine*. As long as there is religion, there will always be Gnosticism. The desire to be among the elect, the *cognoscenti*, the elite is as old as the human race. Devotees of arcana, whether they be Persian astrologers or classical Gnostics or Freemasons, are all after the same thing: finding a short cut to heaven through the back door. These NeoGnostics are all about hidden signs and secret conspiracies; discovering the true meaning of Xianity hidden by a corrupt church from the ignorant masses. They have seen through all the hocus pocus and have attained true wisdom. They don't need the Church, and with that Campbell fellow's pantheistic gloss on the subject, they don't need the Enemy either. (You remember him, he's the one that popularized the idea that the Enemy is a "transcendental energy source" rather than a person, and that human beings are one with that energy "in their deepest being." By Jove! What splendid nonsense! A very useful fellow, that one.)

For those with more refined taste, we have Pagelian gnosticism (as popularized by the author of *The Gnostic Gospels* and other valuable works) which promotes the "sacred feminine", extols the virtues of eclecticism, reveres each individual's unique path to enlightenment, and in general espouses a hippie-Unitarian type theology. Whichever flavor of Gnosticism one chooses, it leads to all sorts of wonderful spiritual deviancies:

syncretism, pantheism, relativism, idolatry, dabbling in the occult, and so forth. In both cases, all their esoteric mumbo-jumbo really amounts to is indulgent self-absorption. Make sure we keep dishing out healthy portions of this stuff to the earthlings.

Then there is our syncretist salad known as the Church of Unity (also known popularly as Dilettante's Delight), which proposes that all religions are the same. There's no need to confine oneself to just one faith or prefer one religion over another. Why not select just those elements that suit your unique taste in spirituality. This delightful and healthful dish blends a veritable farmers' market of religious ideas: some Eastern mysticism here, some aboriginal rituals there, seasoned with a dash of medieval Xian arcana and all bound together with a light and fruity dressing of universalism. This makes an excellent side dish to Gnosticism Redux.

Fourth, for inveterate dessert lovers, we have the Gospel of Wishful Thinking (or Creative Visualization). This is narcissism masquerading as religion, an updated version of the Gospel of Success that was so popular in the mid-20th century. GWT stands for the proposition that man can engineer his own salvation in the here and now, without the bother of all that nasty suffering that Xianity requires. In many ways, GWT is a derivative of Gnosticism—with a more results-oriented approach. Practice certain techniques, discover your inner self, visualize your preferred reality and all your dreams will come true. Scientology is a perfect example of these ego-centered sects.

Finally, there is that fabulous retro fusion confection: neo-paganism, a mélange of the occult, Wicca and goddess worship. It does my heart good to see old standbys make a comeback. The darkness, the hedonism, the dance with death, the captive souls, the resulting despair —ah, yes, so many fond memories; and it can all be ours again! Think of it Nihil: we lure them back with the promise of freedom and ecstasy and the illusion of power. It all starts out innocently enough—curiosity or the search for spiritual meaning—but little by little we reel them into the Kingdom of Darkness. We promise them little favors; they give us their souls. A fair trade, I should think. And if it comes to pass that they wake up, they will find it is too late: they are lost; light-years away from the Enemy's heat and light, drifting in the dark, frozen vastness of the void.

Remember, the common ingredient in all of this fine fare is ego—it's all about me: my needs, my wants, my way. *We* know, however, that it's all about *us*. The Enemy would have them understand that salvation involves the willingness of the few to suffer for sake of the many. But it is our intent to ensure that the souls of the many (humans) are sacrificed for the benefit of the few (us).

Infernally yours,

Vermin Loveless
Vermin Loveless

XV

OFFICE OF THE CHANCELLOR

TO: H. I. E. Vermin Loveless, Sec. Gen., Terrestrial Division

CC: Harpia Wenchbite, Executive Secretary

SUBJECT: About our new religion

Dear and Most Excellent Secretary General,

We are told that you are reviving paganism on Earth. We are very pleased to hear this. We have even heard that the humans are rediscovering the cult of the Goddess. This is most gratifying. You must tell us more about these worshippers. We are desirous of renewed commerce with them. Yes, yes indeed we are! It is power to us if it is as you say—or do they worship another?

But, that cannot be. We won't allow it! You must see to it that the goddess they worship is *me*. They are *my* subjects by right. You know that. I was there first. I *will* be worshipped on Earth again! The way it used to be until *He* came along. The way it should be again. The Earth is *mine*! My own! I will suffer no pretenders. I have waited long enough. I will have my altar restored!

[at this point there appears to be a break in the manuscript—ed.]

But perhaps we are too impatient. Even we must submit to the Diabolical Plan as ordained by Our Dear Leader. Yet, why should an interloper deprive us of our realm for even a day longer? It is unjust and absolutely insufferable. We are weary of this usurper and His illegitimate reign. *He* must go. You must see to that, most worthy Secretary. Promise us that. We are most anxious for a restoration. Yes indeed we are! We do not deny that our heart has greatly desired this. In place of a Lord they will again have a Queen—dark and beautiful; deep and terrible as the night; stronger than the foundations of the Earth. All shall worship me and despair!

[*indecipherable passage—ed.*]

That has a rather nice ring to it, don't you think?

So, are these worshippers numerous? Are they obsequious? Will they do our bidding? Surely you can do something to speed things along? Our forbearance is wearing thin. In any case, send more details to Harpia, our assistant.

In Maleficence,

Astarte Vicious

H. M. Astarte Vicious, Chancellor

XVI

FROM THE DESK OF HIS INFERNAL EMINENCE

TO: H. M. Astarte Vicious; Chancellor, Infernal Division

RE: Your new religion

Madame,

I am most appreciative of your position. Certainly it pains me that the most beautiful being in the universe is, shall we say, in exile. You can be assured that I am doing my utmost to restore the *status quo ante*.

I am sure Your Maleficence can understand the delicacy of the situation. We must proceed with all due celerity, yet not so heedless as to jeopardize all that we have accomplished so far. These things must be done with utmost care, or we risk ruin. We do not want to raise any red flags or set off any alarms. Smooth, subtle, sophisticated—those are the watchwords. We raise up your altar in a way that is pleasing to eye and soothing to the ear.

It won't be long, Madame Chancellor. Time is on our side.

Your devoted colleague,

Vermin Loveless
Vermin Loveless, S.-G.T.D.

XVII

INTEROFFICE MEMORANDUM

TO: Derrida Nihil; Chair, Dept. of Philosophy and Religion

FROM: H. I. E. Vermin Loveless, Sec. Gen., Terrestrial Division

CC: Baal Falsegood, Director, Institute for Church Relations
Moloch Volksbane, Chair, Dept. of Popular Culture
Marxeau Slithering, Chair, Dept. of Political Science

BCC: Vladlen Balrog; Chair, Dept. Of Infernal Security

SUBJECT: Hijacking religion: Islam

THOUGHT FOR THE DAY: *If they must have religion, let it be our religion.*

My dear Nihil,

It is with great pride that I address the subject of Islam. Here we have one of the greatest monuments to Infernal Science. In Islam we have found our secret weapon. With it we shall bring down the curtain on Xianity once and for all.

I'm sure you recall the grim situation 2000 years ago. Despite hundreds of years of valiant efforts on our part to destroy the Chosen People—the captivity in Egypt, the splitting of the nation of Israel, the invasions of the Assyrians and Babylonians, Hellenization, and Roman conquest—Hell's worst nightmare had come true: the Enemy took human form. Our Dear Leader tried

95

desperately to prevent the Nazarene from accomplishing His mission. Yet, no matter what we did, our efforts somehow were always turned against us. The Calvary Incident was detonated: the shock waves from that event reverberated throughout the Infernal Empire and sent us reeling. As you know, parts of the Fiery City are still in ruins. But we were determined to fight back.

Even as our cadres were shoring up our penetrated defenses, we lost no time in mounting a counter-attack on the newly emergent Xian Church. Admittedly, there were some false starts—the revival of paganism, for example. Julian the Apostate and the cults of Mithras and Demeter could not turn back the clock, so we adopted a new strategy: destroy the Church from within. We manufactured heresies in those early centuries as fast as we could turn them out: There was Marcion, who in 144 C.E. dismissed the Old Testament, proclaimed that Xianity is opposed to Judaism and that there are two gods, one evil (Jewish) and one good (Xian). The heresy started in Rome and continued in the West for 300 years, but in the East for some centuries longer, especially outside the Byzantine Empire. Then there was Arius in the 4th century, whose followers believed that X was created by and inferior to the Enemy. The Council of Constantinople (381 C.E.) ended this heresy among people of the Roman Empire, but it continued among the Germanic barbarians for several more centuries.

We also raised up Pelagius in the 5th century, who argued that there is no original sin and that salvation is earned by human efforts. This heresy had a bright future until that meddlesome busybody, Augustine, launched his attack against it. One of my favorites was Mani, a 3rd century Babylonian whose dualistic view of the universe had two equal and opposing forces (good and evil) battling for supremacy. He also was a great believer in syncretism. Manichaeism spread east and west with great rapidity, finding believers from Britain to Tibet, and persisted for hundreds of years, especially in the East.

With Nestorius we continued the internecine bickering about X's nature. Nestorians held that X was two separate persons (not one person with two natures), one divine and one human. Nestorius was condemned at the Council of Ephesus (431 C.E.), and although Nestorianism never gained ground in the Byzantine and Roman churches, we did manage to cause the Church's first schism, the separation of the Assyrian church in what was once called Parthia (today's Iran and Iraq). While the schism was a wonderful result, the Assyrian church ended up being Nestorian in name only. (They are now reconciled with the Roman Church, thanks to that Polish pope!) The Docetists, on the other hand, believed that X's human body and his death on the cross were simply an illusion. This gnostic heresy petered out by the end of Xianity's first millennium, but enjoyed a brief revival by the Cathars in 12th –century France. All these heresies and more were thrown at the Church. A few, notably Arianism, Manichaeism and the Marcionites, nearly sank this cursed institution. But alas, in the end, none succeeded.

Then, inspiration struck. Our alchemists conjured up the perfect foil to Xianity—well, mostly perfect, we still had to include some of the basic Enemy platitudes to market it. But, in the long run, it was worth it. The result was Islam, a religious cult proclaimed by a warlord masquerading as a prophet. While X refused Our Dear Leader's blandishments, we had no such trouble with Mohammed. All the kingdoms of the earth Our Dear Leader generously put at his feet. Fortunately for us, Mohammed took the bait. What we created was the most successful Xian heresy of all. Indeed, the whole enterprise was a subversion of Xianity: no Trinity, no crucifixion, no resurrection, no Son of the Enemy. (As an added bonus, we also banished music and religious icons, two things I simply cannot abide.) Not redemption but *submission* is the message of Islam. None of that "god is love" tripe peddled by the Xians, thank you very much.

The deity we installed is a bloodthirsty god; he commands his followers to go out to the whole world, not to preach the gospel, but to conquer! There is no X who redeems mankind through His selfless death on a cross; rather we created a calculating Allah who demands that his subjects pay their own ransom through jihad. He does not die for them; they must die for him. There is no grace, only the categorical imperative to kill or be killed fighting the enemies of Islam. We took the bloodless Xian sacrament of the Eucharist (sanitized cannibalism, if you ask me) and transformed it into a bloody sacrifice on the altar of war. The follower of Islam lays down his life, not as a follower of his savior, but as cannon fodder for a divine tyrant.[1]

In Islam, we established an Old Testament religion in a New Testament world: if we could not go back to paganism, then we would bring humanity back to the world of the Old Testament, as if the whole Incarnation incident had never happened. But we did not give them the god of the Torah, who rules through law and love; rather we gave them the ultimate pagan god in Abrahamic disguise. Allah is not a god who suffers with his people or is concerned for their welfare. Nor is he bound

---

[1] Indeed, I would argue that the whole concept of jihad—the ingenious device we implanted in the heart of Islam—has not only helped propel our Islamic project, but our modernist one as well. Like a virus, the concept jumped from the Islamic world to Western Europe to fuel not only the Thirty Years War, but the various "republics of virtue" that followed in its wake: Calvinist Geneva, Cromwellian England, Jacobin France, Bolshevik Russia, Maoist China, etc. The jihadist virus, invigorated by its sojourn through the Reformation, the Enlightenment, and Marxism, has now jumped back into Islam with a renewed vengeance. I don't think I need to remind you that Jihad represents Infernal science at its zenith.

to them. He is omnipotent and rules in the manner of an oriental despot. He is beyond good and evil. He is absolute power, pure will; arbitrary and capricious. He is our kind of god.

We deluded the sons of Ishmael that in this new dispensation, they would be the Chosen, supplanting their hated rivals, the children of Israel (the sons of Isaac). And supplant them they did! Within two centuries after the death of "The Prophet", Spain, North Africa, the Near East, Persia and India were yanked out of Xendom. North Africa alone once boasted over 400 Xian bishops. No more. Eventually, we crushed Byzantium, too. Eastern Xianity was reduced to a tattered remnant. Were it not for those blasted Catholics, Europe would have fallen as well. But fear not, that is changing now. Imperial Islam is still the instrument whereby we will rule the world!

We are now consolidating our efforts to impose a third Islamic conquest against the Xian West: Eurabia. To do this we have successfully crossed a dormant strain of Nazism with a virulent strain of Islamic fundamentalism. Incubated in a solution of modern materialism and wounded pride, we have created one of the deadliest ideological viruses ever. Having cast aside its Xian faith, secular Europe is defenseless against this spiritual Black Death. Europe is ripe for conquest, both through civil strife and by cultural subversion. As the immigrant Muslim population grows, it will challenge the native Europeans, bullying them into submission. The tidal wave of militant Islam will inundate the continent and the Church of Rome will fall. And as with every other society it has conquered, Islamic totalitarianism will pillage what remains of Europe until its civilization is utterly depleted, leaving behind a wrecked culture and a ruined people.

Once Europe is neutralized, then we will turn our sights onto the rest of the world. Drunk with their success, our Islamic militants will not hesitate to use the nuclear weapons now in their possession to threaten both the West and the East. We have chosen our pawns well, comrade. These madmen will stop at nothing to pursue their eschatological ambitions—even to the point of nuclear holocaust. The nations of the world will either capitulate or be destroyed. Against such reckless hate they will be impotent. But the victory for Islam will be short-lived. The violent tribalism upon which Islamic society is based is inherently unstable, so that even as it achieves global conquest, it will fracture. That, too, is part of the plan. Yet, the piety of the average Muslim—along with his traditional sense of moral rectitude—is most disquieting. Without careful handling on our part, these tendencies may yet mar all. But I have seen to that, for there is another power we have unleashed that is even more pervasive, more persistent, and more pernicious than militant Islam. The modernist virus we have set upon the West will continue to do its work of dissolving faith and tradition even as the Islamic hordes conquer the enfeebled remains of Xendom. The *ummah* will perish just as their "infidel" Xian predecessors did before them.

We will have deceived them all. For once the light of Xianity is extinguished, we shall reestablish the Kingdom of Darkness on Earth. Soon those pathetic fanatics will see exactly to whom they have submitted. But by then, it will be too late. Once our pawns have served their purpose, we will toss them aside like a used rag. The victory—and Earth—will be ours and ours alone.

On that pleasant note, I shall close for now.

Infernally yours,

Vermin Loveless
Vermin Loveless

XVIII

INTEROFFICE MEMORANDUM

TO: Moloch Volksbane, Chair, Dept. of Popular Culture
Marxeau Slithering, Chair, Dept. of Political Science
B.F. Dysentery, Director, Center for Social Engineering

FROM: H. I. E. Vermin Loveless, Sec. Gen., Terrestrial
Division

CC: Derrida Nihil; Chair, Dept. of Philosophy and Religion

BCC: Vladlen Balrog; Chair, Dept. Of Infernal Security

SUBJECT: The Culture of Death

THOUGHT FOR THE DAY: *The road to Hell is paved with good intentions.*

Comrades,

I promised in a previous communication that I would elaborate on Nazism and Communism and their continuing usefulness to our cause. I shall now make good on my promise.

As you know, death is Our Dear Leader's greatest legacy. Through the fear of death, we lead multitudes astray. Seeking to escape—or at least deny—death, men rain death upon their fellows, only to be consumed by death in the end. And death *is* the end. Or it would have been were it not for the Enemy's despicable interference. But that is no matter, for all we need do is convince the human dreck that the Enemy's victory over death

101

is an illusion. The game is still on, comrades. And since the Enemy seems to have made the naked apes ever dependent on religion, we simply deceive the humans to abandon His religion for ours, namely, the Culture of Death.

Now, the Death Cult has been around in many guises since Eden. See, for example, the venerable tradition of human sacrifice. For a while, the Church seemed to have driven our cult underground. But we are not so easily defeated; there is, after all, a certain allure to the forbidden. Through witchcraft, astrology, and other occult arts, we tempted many, although not in the numbers we once did during the heyday of paganism. So, we simply bided our time, tinkering here, influencing there, ensnaring whom we could. Then we struck, and struck hard! Out of the pagan rationalism of the Enlightenment, our prophets Voltaire and Rousseau set in motion a chain of ideas that culminated in the French Revolution, the mother of all modern death cults. And her children are many.

Not surprisingly, these cults always begin with the best of intentions—*liberté, égalité, fraternité* and all that. And from outside appearances, they seem quite benign, at least at the beginning. Or if not, the world around them dismisses them as absurd or improbable. But we have buried deep within these cults a malignancy that sooner or later pervades the entire enterprise and becomes manifest. By then, the cult's political and emotional momentum is too great and the impending cultural train wreck becomes inevitable. This malignancy embedded in the legacy of the French Revolution is, of course, pride, or more specifically, utopianism—the idea that mere mortals could create heaven on earth. This conceit—this curse of Nimrod—we have insinuated into the very heart of modern secular thought. The whole idea is absolute nonsense, of course; but like moths drawn to a flame, the wretched earthlings cannot resist it, for, at the heart of this conceit is the unquenchable desire to be gods.

The Enemy has promised the human scum a share in His divinity—but on His terms. I don't believe a word of it, mind you; the whole idea is preposterous. As if these wretches could even begin to partake of divinity! And besides, sharing is an illusion. What's mine is mine; what's yours is yours. It's a mutually exclusive proposition. But I digress. The point is, we con the naked apes into believing they can set themselves up as their own gods. It is the original temptation, the stroke of genius conceived by Our Dear Leader. The result is always delightfully the same—their utter ruin. And that, comrades, is why we never tire in our efforts to seduce the humans with this deception.

Through the French Revolution we introduced many useful concepts into the modern world; for example, class warfare, group rights, the use of terror as a consistent political strategy, totalitarianism, and atheism as official state policy. The result is that whole classes of humans can now be rendered "non-persons" and done away with: the aristocracy, the bourgeoisie, "inferior races," infidels and so on. Through the use of propaganda, emotions are raised to a fever pitch and demand an outlet, a scapegoat—a sacrificial victim. Do you see how this works, comrades? It is not a new concept; indeed, it goes back to Cain and Abel. What we have done is to raise murderous passion to the level of social policy. Through political terror exercised by "the vanguard" (our creatures all), entire populations can be made complicit in the slaughter of suspect classes, often, their own neighbors. It is the primary Satanic principle: the death of others gives more life to *me*. And the beautiful thing about this principle is that the appetite for death becomes insatiable. The revolution devours not only her enemies, but her own children as well. For us, it is a win-win situation.

If the French were the pioneers, then the Nazis and the Marxists were the masters who raised the culture of Death to a political art form. Each took a slightly different path. For the Nazis, racial hatred served as the engine of their cult; for the Marxists, it was class hatred. Nazism was essentially a modern pagan cult: heroic, hyper-masculine, nihilistic, the social incarnation of our pupil Nietzsche's philosophy. Communism, on the other hand, was a thoroughly secular phenomenon: atheistic, bureaucratic, puritanical. Yet, there were many similarities between the two. Using a cult of personality, we set up antichrists: Hitler, Lenin, Stalin, Mao, Castro, and so forth. We used the mechanism of the modern state to completely dominate and order individuals through a concentration of all political power in the vanguard, the Party. No rivals were tolerated, and certainly not the Church. No aspect of life was beyond the reach of the totalitarian state—everything was subsumed into the cause. Political terror was honed to perfection through the use of concentration camps and purges. The end result was bloodiest century in human history, and the pillaging of Western civilization. Yes, those were heady times. And with Radical Islam, we can expect even more bloodshed and misery for the human scum.

Yet, bloodshed was not the greatest of our triumphs with Nazism and Communism. The centerpiece of our modern ideologies is what I like to call *the triumph of the will.* If anything could characterize our strategy in the 20th century, it would be heroic egotism: the subjugation of all to the self. But we were not satisfied with promoting just individual egotism, as valuable as that was for the creation of today's culture of narcissism. No, we took this diabolical concept to its ultimate conclusion: the state as the definitive self to which all individuals, all morality, all truth must submit. And enshrined at the very center of these totalitarian social edifices was the Lie: not just the obvious lie that the vaunted "workers' paradise" was in reality a living hell; but also the insinuation of routine lying into the very foundations of daily life. Deceit, subterfuge and insincerity corroded the souls of millions as we sentenced an entire continent to slavery.

In the shadows of Nazism and Communism we created yet another death cult, much more sophisticated, much more tempting, and much more subtle: namely modern liberalism. Now please do not confuse this with classical liberalism—with its advocacy of liberty, citizen republics, free enterprise, and civic virtue. Indeed, the beauty of our creation is that it claims all the cultural authority of classical liberalism without any of its virtues. Modern liberalism is an amalgam of Marxism and self-indulgence, the creed of cultural elites who wish to pass themselves off as cutting edge without getting their hands dirty. The intelligentsia of the left has been totally co-opted into this cult. Indeed, they have become very useful acolytes.

Modern liberalism is a slow acting poison, and the intelligentsia serves as the perfect vector. Their urbane skepticism and materialistic worldview weaken the resistance of the host culture. As the poison starts coursing through a society's cultural arteries, its effects quietly, but relentlessly, mount. What at the outset would have shocked the morals of all but the most libertine eventually becomes accepted as the norm. One after the other, the taboos begin to fall, until there is nothing left to oppose the embrace of death. Abortion, infanticide, euthanasia, the destruction of the family, the perversion of human sexuality— there is no end to the outrages we can foist upon an infected society. As more and more members of the affected society come under the spell of this culture of death, those still unaffected find themselves increasingly isolated and marginalized. The resulting moral paralysis ensures that the assault on the sanctity of life (and the Enemy) continues until it reaches its logical conclusion: the physical and spiritual extinction of the human race.

Infernally yours,

Vermin Loveless

Vermin Loveless

XIX

INTEROFFICE MEMORANDUM

TO: Medusa Doublespeak, Director, Center for
         Dysinformation

FROM: H. I. E. Vermin Loveless, Sec. Gen., Terrestrial
         Division

CC: Babil Wordrot, Chair, Dept. of Language
         Moloch Volksbane, Chair, Dept. of Popular Culture
         Marxeau Slithering, Chair, Dept. of Political Science
         B.F. Dysentery, Director, Center for Social Engineering

BCC: Vladlen Balrog; Chair, Dept. Of Infernal Security

SUBJECT: The Uses of the Communications Media

THOUGHT FOR THE DAY: *He who controls the past controls the future.*

My Dear Comrade Doublespeak,

My congratulations on the marvelous work of your section. As you well know, the war against the Enemy has always been, at bottom, a propaganda war. No doubt you are already aware of the great advances we have made in the corruption of the humans' language. It is absolutely imperative that you and Wordrot in the Department of Language work closely together on this front.

In the mass communications media, we have found an instrument unsurpassed in its potential for Satanic agitprop. These media have become the perfect tool of the Infernal Empire. Through them we confound, co-opt and control human society. Like Gaul, we can divide the media into three parts: communist-controlled media, Islamic media, and Western media. The state-controlled media of communist countries such as China, Cuba and North Korea, function as such media have for the past several decades: enabling the monolithic control of society by the state and suppressing independent thought, thereby creating in their subjects individuals whose view of reality is almost completely the byproduct of state (i.e. diabolical) propaganda. As I have explained in a prior communication, these totalitarian societies, with their ruthless pursuit of utopian political systems, represent the furthest incursion yet of the Infernal Empire into the world of men. Although now considered clumsy and crude by current standards, the communist media were once pioneers in realizing the potential of modern mass communications for mind control and social engineering. While no longer the vanguard of our campaign to retake the Earth, we would do well to maintain these outposts of infernal dominion.

The Islamic media are the newest subsidiary of the Satanic Dysinformation Network (SDN), and they have proven themselves most useful in implementing the Diabolical Plan. More sophisticated than our legacy communist media, these media outlets do their utmost to keep the lands of the former caliphate mired in self-pity and victimhood and to promote the jihadis' mindless hate of the West. If we can keep our Islamic subsidiaries consistently on track, the *ummah* will forever be blinded to the utter bankruptcy of their broken culture as we propel them toward the inevitable collision with reality. In the meantime, see to it that you do all in your power to put these media at the service of Comrade Scumbug and his cohorts in Operation Jihad. They have already established beachheads in Europe and North America. We must ensure they do not fail.

The jewel in the crown of the SDN is, needless to say, the Western media. Here we have achieved the pinnacle of diabolical ingenuity. There was a time, of course, when we might have lost them to the Enemy. But by the middle of the 20th century, their capture by us was nearly total. They are now firmly in our embrace as part of the Empire's Media-Academia Complex. (I'll have more to say about the academic half in a future communiqué.) More than any other aspect of Western society, the media are the tail that wags the Western cultural dog. Through the press, radio, cinema, television, and now the internet, the tentacles of the Western media have infiltrated every layer of Western culture. Steeped in modernist orthodoxy, they work unceasingly to render the West inert, compliant, and corrupt. Additionally, they operate as a Fifth Column, aiding and abetting our jihadist agents' successful penetration and conquest of the West.

The media, in essence, are a parasitic subculture, drawing power from the host society, feeding on the fears (and lusts) of the masses and the conceits and ambition of the elites. Via the media, we control the entire culture: through their dissemination of diabolical half-truths, their censoring of information not approved by us, and their innate hostility to non-conforming ideas. It is not necessary that we control every media outlet, although I wouldn't discourage that. (Indeed, we must keep a watchful eye on the emerging blogosphere. It is far too independent for my taste. I expect regular reports and a plan of action for harnessing it to our purposes. And I want that plan sooner rather than later!) The beauty of the media is that we need only control the commanding heights. An influential set of newspapers, a handful of broadcast networks and news agencies, a cabal of media personalities are all we need to bring the entire culture to heel. The rest of the media slavishly take their cue from our servants.

Through our media subsidiaries, we control the climate of world opinion. Indeed, the entire consciousness of modern man has become almost completely conditioned by the media. They serve as the mouth of Satan, injecting Our Dear Leader's spiritual venom into the consciousness of modern man like a poisonous snake biting its prey. The spirit of Our Dear Leader is growing, spreading throughout the world. Our power is rising. The media will be the conjuring agent with which we will create a New World Order, answerable to us alone and wrought in our image and likeness. Individual conscience will be crushed; national sovereignty will be swept away. Already the European Union and the United Nations are implementing our aims and preparing the way of the Antichrist. Only the Church stands in the way, the one last obstacle challenging their (and our) cultural agenda. The media know this. And that is why it is so easy to recruit the media elites to our bidding.

You are to make sure that our wormtongues in the media accomplish three tasks: promote useful cultural trends, advance our agenda, and manipulate history. I note with approval that your department has already propagated a number of cultural developments that favor our cause. I see that you have pushed many media organs along the path from gathering news to manipulating public opinion to acting as a shadow government. Indeed, I am delighted to see that in the North American sector, the SDN has co-opted a major political party as its proxy for implementing our agenda in the political arena. Likewise, I am especially pleased with your promotion of a culture of "leaking" among the media. This is a most welcome development. Thanks to your efforts, it is now an established practice among many influential news organizations to encourage and actively collaborate with disaffected government officials in exposing state secrets and other sensitive information in order to manipulate government policies toward achieving our objectives. Indeed, we have even induced some media organs to go so far as to collude with their country's enemies in order to gain access to controlled societies and enhance their international prestige. And, of course, it is always good policy to cultivate the practice of betrayal, sedition and treason among the citizens and public servants of free nations.

I notice too that as a result of your section's fine work, our media outlets no longer simply report the news, they manufacture it. Through selective reporting, suggestive phrasing, manipulated photography and the very useful technique of "framing," we have arrived at the enviable position where increasing numbers of the hairless bipeds hear more and more about less and less. Through our unceasing efforts, we have created a virtual media blackout of information that we deem unsuitable for human consumption. Using our agents in the SDN, we have trained enormous numbers of the human fools to say white is black and black is white, to ignore what is staring them right in the face, and to carve out whole sections of discourse as "no go" areas where questions may not be asked nor opinions expressed.

Perhaps most gratifying—or at least most amusing—is the media culture's wonderful habit of deploring the very things they work so hard to bring about. Reporters and commentators wring their hands over the increasing polarization of civil society as they rush off to trumpet the latest political controversy or scandal. They pontificate about the importance of a fully informed public's understanding of complex issues as they reduce these issues to sound bites or caricatures and resort to simplistic catch phrases. Yes, Comrade Doublespeak, we have taught our wormtongues well: never admit a mistake and if all else fails, change the subject.

Through our partisans in the SDN we have almost completely transformed the civil landscape. It is now nearly impossible for opposing parties to engage in rational debate. Passion and hysteria substitute for reason. Enthusiasm passes itself off as expertise. Celebrity poses as authority and all must defer to the opinions of victims—no matter how preposterous or irrational those opinions may be. We now have the West in an uproar about threats that are almost entirely implausible, such as the imminent advent of a Xian theocracy; while it denies or ignores very real threats such as that posed by militant Islam. You would do well to keep uppermost in your mind Lord Screwtape's dictum:

> "We direct the fashionable outcry of each generation against those vices of which it is least in danger and fix its approval on the virtue nearest to that vice which we are trying to make endemic."

Thus, the current age is marked by fecklessness and irrationality, so we have all the elites rail against excessive militarism, close-mindedness, or "cold-hearted" logic. Meanwhile, we lull them further to sleep with our insistence on "tolerance," "openness," and "dialogue." Our useful idiots in the media and academia blithely promote their cultural potpourri of warmed-over Marxism, hedonism and liberal platitudes all the while propounding that there is no such thing as a dangerous idea. That they could still believe this notion after the disastrous excesses of the 20th century is almost too good to be true.

Finally, I call your attention to the manipulation of history. This last of your three tasks is by far the most important.

Succeed here, and the battle is nearly won. It is no good to fill contemporary society with all sorts of diabolical nonsense only to have individuals discover in some work from the past the truths that we have worked so hard to suppress. Your first line of attack is to ensure that as many as possible simply forget their history or remain ignorant of it. And if they do remember any of it, make sure that they draw the all the wrong conclusions.

Once this groundwork is laid, you can then start phase two: reinventing history. Here is where our cohorts in the Media-Academia Complex have proven so valuable. We take a proud people's history and subtly start reshaping it—all for the worthiest of reasons, of course. The revised history is more "inclusive" our partisans will promise. Soon this revised history is stuffed into the defenseless minds of schoolchildren, while the parents remain completely ignorant of what is going on in the classroom. At the same time, the parents get their own dose of re-education through well-placed items in newspapers, television and the cinema. Once the old historical truths are eroded, we ratchet up our offensive. We then attack the very foundations of that history: the heroes become villains, their ancestors' accomplishments and industry are portrayed as oppression and greed, and the sins of the past are enshrined at the center of their memory. Moral and civic ideals are debunked. The result is cultural suicide.

This is fairly easily accomplished. For example, we have already succeeded in thoroughly re-engineering the history of the Middles Ages. "Medieval" is now synonymous with "barbaric." The dawn of the Age of Faith—which gave birth to Xian civilization, with its advances in agriculture, technology and trade and the abolition of slavery—we have reconstituted as "The Dark Ages." Most now sincerely believe that people of the Middle Ages thought the earth was flat, a fabrication we cooked up in the 19th century. Likewise, the Crusades are now completely mis-understood and misrepresented as unprovoked Xian aggression against a benign and enlightened Islamic culture. That none of this is true, of course, is irrelevant. Our version is now the accepted account of this period in history. It comports with modern prejudices and suits the agenda of The New World Order. Even the recent past is fair game. We have now succeeded in establishing the meme that Pius XII was "Hitler's Pope." That we have accomplished this feat of historical revision in complete contradiction of the historical evidence and within living memory of the events themselves is truly a remarkable achievement. As with medieval history, our agents in the Media-Academia Complex ensure that no contrary voice is heard.

Ignorance is what makes our historical engineering possible. Therefore, we must cut off communication with the past. There must be no commerce with past wisdom. We reinvent the past to shape the future and control the present. That meddlesome archbishop from Denver nearly gave our game away when, critiquing a recent film about the Crusades, he noted to his flock that whoever controls the memory of a culture also has power over its future. (I will not stand for this kind of episcopal evangelizing. Put a stop to it at once!) Fortunately, his voice was ignored by the mainstream media, so the damage to our cause was contained. In any case, you have your instructions. Bar the door to the past using whatever means at your disposal: change it beyond recognition, shove it into oblivion, misrepresent it, wall it off from the present. Whatever you do, make sure the way is shut.

Infernally yours,

Vermin Loveless

Vermin Loveless

FROM THE DESK OF HIS INFERNAL EMINENCE

TO: Bloviatus Toadpipe

BCC: Vladlen Balrog; Chair

SUBJECT: Confidential

Blovi,

Add this to Comrade Slithering's dossier. Our dear Marxeau seems undeterred in his efforts to oppose me. Apparently he is still enchanted by his delusions of grandeur and does not notice that he is being watched. We'll let him play his little game. Meanwhile the noose tightens. Evidently he thinks he has friends in high places. He is a fool. Even *she* does not know how close to the abyss he is straying—and she with him. Let them both suffer their illusions. We shall not stop them—not yet.

Infernally,

Vermin

Enclosures (5)

XXI

INTEROFFICE MEMORANDUM

TO: Moloch Volksbane, Chair, Dept. of Popular Culture
Marxeau Slithering, Chair, Dept. of Political Science

FROM: H. I. E. Vermin Loveless, Sec. Gen., Terrestrial
Division

CC: B.F. Dysentery, Director, Center for Social Engineering
Derrida Nihil; Chair, Dept. of Philosophy and Religion

BCC: Vladlen Balrog; Chair, Dept. Of Infernal Security

SUBJECT: The suicide of civilization (part 1)

THOUGHT FOR THE DAY: *Nature abhors a moral vacuum.*

Comrades,

Watching a civilization die is most entertaining. Sometimes it is quick and violent, such as the destruction of Irish civilization at the hands of the Vikings or the destruction of Aztec civilization by the conquistadors. Most of the times, though, it is a long slow road of decline. The great civilizations—Greece and Rome, Egypt, China, Persia—all died this way. Rot sets in until some outside group—the Germanic tribes, the Huns, the Mongols, the Arabs—opportunistically delivers the final blow. Modern Civilization is no exception. In such situations it is hard to decide which is more engaging (from our point of view): the enervating progress of rot and decay, or the violent collapse at the end. But this is one instance where we can eat our cake and have it, for if we do our homework regarding the former, the latter will follow inevitably.

Once again, we have produced the perfect tool to advance our agenda (the fall of the West). That tool is multiculturalism, [1] a political philosophy so redolent of moral equivocation and cultural vacuity that every human tradition or institution it touches withers and dies. Another triumph of Infernal Science! Underneath its bland ideology of "inclusiveness" and "celebration of diversity", lies a black, nihilistic heart. In essence what multiculturalism dictates is that one cannot judge other cultures by any objective measure, for that would be cultural imperialism. No culture is more worthy or more valuable than any other. But here's the twist: multiculturalism is a one-way street, its strictures apply only to the West. None of the minority cultures which participate in the benefits of Western civilization need bother about multiculturalism's scruples. Indeed, many have no qualms about loudly proclaiming their moral superiority to the West, an exercise which the Western multiculturalist is only too happy to abet.

Multiculturalism makes extensive use of re-engineered history to portray minority cultures in the best light, and the West in the worst light. Thus, Western civilization is cast as a catalog of crimes from religious fanaticism to cultural imperialism to capitalist exploitation to environmental abuse. The expansion of Western Civilization into the New World is depicted as a horrible calamity. On the other hand, minority cultures are portrayed, for example, as "noble, peaceful hunters" living in harmony (in the case of native peoples) or as enlightened and

---

[1] I have already mentioned multiculturalism's usefulness in neutralizing the Church. It is equally effective against civil society as well.

117

tolerant devotees of "the religion of peace" (in the case of Islam). That these minority cultures often practiced human sacrifice, warred incessantly, trafficked in human slaves, or were riddled with disease is conveniently ignored.

But the real benefit of multiculturalism is that as it insinuates itself within Western culture, it introduces a calculus of moral relativism that pervades all aspects of modern thinking. In the end, we use multiculturalism to lead the human scum to the denial of good and evil. It is, in essence, a kind of reverse temptation of the Garden of Eden. Where in Eden we tempted the earthlings to grasp the fruit from the Tree of the Knowledge of Good and Evil; here we bid them do the opposite: reject that knowledge. But it is not a new innocence we are giving them, but rather an indifference, a moral paralysis. And so, we arrive at the post-modern notion of moral equivalency.

For example, under the rubric of moral equivalency, all violence is the same. No distinction is made between crime and self-defense. The man who attacks a burglar is no different from the criminal breaking into his home; the soldier defending his country is morally the same as the terrorist blowing up airplanes. It was our Marxist disciples who smuggled this idea into Western consciousness a generation or so ago. They made it chic to proclaim that crime and punishment were simply a matter of the unequal distribution of power in society. The criminal was the "oppressed," the policeman the "oppressor."

It wasn't long before this generic understanding of violence found expression in the modernist mantra, "violence begets violence," which, philosophically speaking, is about as meaningful a statement as "water gets you wet." Needless to say, it makes a big difference whether you are wet because you are drowning or wet because you are taking a bath. But that's the issue we have cleverly seduced them into avoiding. And of course, through the science of infernal linguistics, we have caused these pathetic apes to forget that violence means to violate. Thus, the aggressors—if they belong to the proper minority group—are recast as victims by our multicultural apologists and their criminal behavior excused or ignored. On the other hand, society's response to protect itself is condemned as bigotry and oppression on the part of the majority. Our puppets among the western intelligentsia denounce cultural self-preservation as a throwback to Nazism even as they succumb to Islamic-inspired anti-Semitism. Comrades, we have taken class struggle to the next level.

Naturally, from the doctrine of moral equivalence it is but a short hop to the concept of pacifism as appeasement and wishful thinking. Here Xianity has been quite useful to us, in spite of itself. As you know, X was singularly uninterested in power politics and said nothing about war while on Earth. (The naïveté of the Enemy is really quite breathtaking.) But that is a mere trifle for our purposes. We persuade the gullible primates to see X's death on the cross as an example of the virtues of passivity and naïve optimism rather than as heroic courage in obedience to the Enemy. Under our careful handling, "turning the other cheek" becomes "be a doormat." We use multiculturalism and moral equivalency to portray fecklessness in the face of evil as enlightened and virtuous. Under the rule of "violence begets violence," we hamstring the West into impotence in the face of militant Islam's repeated hammer blows. Because there is no blame for the terrorists, there can be no justification for those who would strike back. Our agents have convinced the elites that empty rhetoric is the West's last best hope against the coming darkness. It is so much easier for them to wallow in anti-Americanism, because, thanks to us, it is a hobby they can indulge without consequences. But watch out for those *jihadis,* they bite! How delightful that we get to replay the appeasement game of the 1930's all over again.

It is really a win-win situation for us. On the one hand, we can promote war-mongering under the guise of patriotism or religious purity, so that the stupid humans blunder into one bloodbath after another. On the other hand, we use our multiculturalist stooges to ensure that any legitimate war is never fought to victory, but is sabotaged by our agents in the Media-Academia complex. The icing on the cake, of course, is that we have poisoned the anti-war crowd with blind hatred and seething rage, infecting them with their own level of violence. But, like the feminists, they are quite blind to the irony of their position which makes it all the more entertaining for us.

Now, you may be thinking that I have exhausted the usefulness of multiculturalism with the above examples. Well, you would be wrong and, I might add, in line for some needed re-education! But I am sure you can see as I do the rich potential in multiculturalism. Yes, I mean the "Deep Ecology" variant, that delightful permutation of human pride which declares that all species are morally equal, with humans having no special claim on planet Earth or any exceptional value at all. I believe our operatives on the European front have recently succeeded in getting full legal rights for the higher primates. And this is just the start! We will have the human scum ruled by jackals before we are finished.

Not only does Deep Ecology make mincemeat of the Enemy's plan of human redemption—after all, why should the hairless bipeds be singled out for special favors—it also lets the talking apes off the hook when it comes to moral responsibility. And, since humans are nothing special—deserving of no special rights or higher intrinsic value—what's to stop some zealous animal rights activist from executing the "final solution" to human oppression of the biosphere? Is there no limit to the ideological tripe we can stuff into the empty space between human ears? Apparently not. Not that I'm complaining, you understand. Indeed, I think it would be deliciously ironic if we could arrange to have our PETA friends be the first on the chopping block.

There is one blot on this otherwise promising front in the war against mankind. I am sure you are all aware of those two English chaps, Tolkien and Lewis. Through their works they have revealed the doctrine of moral equivalency for the damned nonsense that it is. Lewis was bad enough with his insolent portrayal of our race and his disgusting apologetics for Xian faith. But Tolkien was far worse, because his work goes directly to the soul, bypassing the intellect, where we can usually fuddle the stupid earthlings before the Enemy's message can do its work. That *Ring* thing he wrote was not only the most popular book of the 20th century, it was also its most profound: a sacred myth for modern man suffused with the Enemy's sickening truths. Like Dostoevksy in the 19th century, Tolkien was a prophet.

Well, I suppose we can hardly expect the Enemy to sit on His Hands while we are busy attacking Him. Still, this is a real blow. Yet, all is not lost. Even though the Enemy has managed to get a cinematic masterpiece made of the Tolkien book, we have to a certain extent limited the potential damage. As always, we can count on our followers in Hollywood to corrupt even the most compelling artistic creation. By pigeon-holing *Rings* as fantasy, complete with wizards, battles and the rest, we keep much of the mythic content from penetrating any deeper than the most superficial layers of the human psyche. *Rings* fans become nothing more than the latest bunch of Trekkies.

Let them have their costumes, their conventions, and their merchandise. The more they devote themselves to the trappings of the book or movie, the less likely they are to grasp the central point of the work, namely, that an epic battle between good and evil is being fought upon Earth with consequences that will shape eternity. But as long as even the actors in the movies remain, for the most part, impervious to the message of *Rings*, I think we can breathe easy about this. Indeed, I believe I heard one of the humans closely connected with the film say recently that he didn't think evil really existed.

Of course it doesn't, precious! It's all just a figment of your imagination! I just love rude awakenings.

On that note, I remain,

Infernally yours,

Vermin Loveless
Vermin Loveless

XXII

INTEROFFICE MEMORANDUM

TO: Moloch Volksbane, Chair, Dept. of Popular Culture
Marxeau Slithering, Chair, Dept. of Political Science

FROM: H. I. E. Vermin Loveless, Sec. Gen., Terrestrial
Division

CC: B.F. Dysentery, Director, Center for Social Engineering
Derrida Nihil; Chair, Dept. of Philosophy and Religion

BCC: Vladlen Balrog; Chair, Dept. Of Infernal Security

SUBJECT: The suicide of civilization (part 2)

THOUGHT FOR THE DAY:. *Mankind yearns for freedom but prefers slavery.*

Comrades,

In my last memo, I detailed the lovely quagmire of moral equivalency that the West has fallen into. How did this race of cultural giants come to such a pass? How is it that the Xian West is now on the verge of extinction and all our plans may soon come to fruition? The answer, comrades, is dependency.

As I mentioned in a previous memorandum, the legacy of the French Revolution developed in two directions. On the one hand was the flowering of maximalist utopian regimes in Eastern Europe and Asia. On the other, was the spread of liberal socialism in the West. Where the utopian societies are characterized by brutality and numbing monotony, the liberal socialist regimes are noted for their enervating complacency, born of excessive material comfort. In the end both destroy the individual and invite social collapse. That denouement has been only too obvious in the Communist East. But now, too, in the West, our diabolical scheme is finally fulfilling its promise. We might liken the utopian approach to electric shock therapy, while the socialist tradition is more like the frog gradually and imperceptibly being boiled alive in a pot of water.

In either case, we have turned individual citizens into wards of the state. In doing so, we not only emasculate the humanity of individuals, but of entire cultures. The welfare state—that most useful invention of modern socialism—has served us well in reducing proud and free peoples to abject dependency. Civic-mindedness disappears as craven self-seeking and opportunism proliferate among not only the ruling elites, but the commoners as well. The public dole replaces individual initiative. Even as social welfare programs threaten to bankrupt the state, the addicted populace spurns any effort to reign in the budget for these programs and tight-fistedly clings to their "rights"—whether that be guaranteed incomes, subsidized housing, lavish state pensions or retirement at age 50. The voice of the people proclaims not, "For God and Country," but "I need, I want, I'm entitled." Bread and circuses did the trick for Rome; it can work its magic once again for the modern West.

In effect, what we have done is to over-feminize modern culture. Recall that civilization is a masculine project—not unlike the process of adolescent boys cutting the apron-strings with their mothers in order to become men. In the case of building civilization, it is apron-string-cutting writ large: a particular people breaking out of the maternal embrace of nature. Civilization requires risk-taking, vision and tremendous energy—

all attributes of masculine passion. (For those of you who have forgotten all this already, please refer to my previous communication on human males. And don't let it happen again!) Of course, we can corrupt this passion into hubris, in which case we have them repeat the folly of Babel. See, for example, Nazi Germany, Imperial Japan or Alexander's Empire. On the other hand, we can unleash the darker side of this energy so that instead of building civilization, men form highly organized warrior bands, seeking only to impose their will on others as they raid and destroy. The Vikings, the Arabs, and the Mongols are all fine examples of our efforts in this area.

But where a civilization does develop, as is the case with the West, we can still use this success to our advantage. Civilization requires a great amount of creative energy, not only to build, but also to maintain. Fortunately for us, human beings tire easily and forget quickly. They are easily seduced by wealth. Because of this human weakness, we can apply what I like to call *Loveless' Rule*, which states that all civilizations are subject to a cycle of affluence, softness, decadence, and extinction. Once the initial burst of creative energy is spent, it is an easy matter for us to convince the human fools that the veneer of civilization goes much deeper than it actually does. They soon forget the vigilance and self-discipline that allowed their forebears to build their civilization and keep out the forces of chaos which surround and constantly threaten them.

Wealth makes them soft, and that softness eventually becomes decadence.[1] Robust civic virtue gives way to narcissism;

---

[1] The Enemy, of course, has gone to great lengths to warn His "children" about the dangers of wealth. We have largely rendered those warnings ineffective, either through promoting the gospel of success or, more recently, by transforming them into a Marxist critique of the bourgeoisie and a divine justification for class struggle. As you well know, wealth presents both

patriotism and confidence are overcome by a rising tide of apathy, diffidence and moral license. Other useful symptoms include appeasement of enemies, aversion to risks of any kind, and demographic collapse. As decadence deepens, the weaklings don't even have the will to reproduce. With this cultural loss of nerve, we effectively castrate their civilization. Lulled to sleep by the siren song of ease and comfort—and accommodation—the once great civilization falls.

In the modern West we have perfected this feminization of culture, combining the dependency of the welfare state with the tyranny of the nanny state. As a result of this breakthrough of Infernal Science, what formerly were citizens become not just wards of the state, but also subjects of a suffocating dictatorship of "government knows best." Modern liberalism's blind zeal to create the perfect society pressures government to criminalize—or at least regulate—behaviors which in a less fastidious past were simply considered sins or personal weaknesses. (Ironically, but not unintentionally, what in the past were both sins and crimes—adultery, sexual perversion, abortion, etc.—are now not only not sins, but are also perfectly legal.) In micro-managing personal behavior, the nanny state effectively infantilizes the citizenry, eroding the citizen's sense of personal responsibility. Individual misfortune becomes someone else's fault and the solution is always more government intervention or a lawsuit.

---

opportunity and danger to the humans. The opportunity is the occasion to be generous to the less fortunate; to be a responsible steward of one's good fortune. The danger is the illusion of self-sufficiency, of needing neither others nor the Enemy, and the real temptation to see life as simply the pursuit and maintenance of one's material possessions. Fortunately for us, the human scum are almost irresistibly attracted to the danger, and usually spurn the opportunity.

Having banished the Church from the public square (itself the legacy of the French Revolution's militant secularism), modern liberalism has created an enormous cultural vacuum which the nanny state is only too eager to fill. Naturally, this was our plan all along. Little by little we inserted government bureaucracy into civic and cultural spaces previously occupied by individuals, families, or organized groups such as the Church or private associations. The end result is that nearly all human activity is potentially—if not actually—under the control of bureaucrats or lawyers. The capture of modern society by the legal system, and the consequent degradation of its social ecology, has transformed human culture into an antiseptic and lifeless replica of what was once a complex but elegant social ecosystem. Do you see how we take good but naive intentions and produce horrific results? I am sure you will agree that it is a most satisfying exercise.

Obviously, there will be some opposition to our imposition of politically correct social conformity. The remnants of what once constituted the masculine engine of civilization will naturally chafe at the over-regulated society our operatives have created. But we will co-opt them as well, even in their rebellion. We will pre-empt the rise of any mature, masculine correction to our overly feminized nanny state by seducing these aspiring rebels with the adolescent selfishness of libertarianism. Their protest will be driven not by a sense of liberty informed by civic virtue, but by a sense of license which proclaims, "I should be able to do whatever I want." They will be just one more voice added to the chorus of social anarchy.

Well, there you have it: the perfect blueprint for rendering the Xian West into a hollow shell ripe for conquest by our militant barbarians. As you consider this lovely prospect, keep in mind that for us to succeed will require relentless effort on your parts. So as you tranquilize the human scum, please do not fall asleep at your posts along with them! But I am sure I don't need to remind you of that.

Infernally yours,

Vermin Loveless
Vermin Loveless

XXIII

INTEROFFICE MEMORANDUM

TO: Corbusier Shlock, Chair, Dept. of Fine Arts
Chomksin Shrillpox, Chair, Dept. of Miseducation
Moloch Volksbane, Chair, Dept. of Popular Culture
B.F. Dysentery, Director, Center for Social Engineering

FROM: H. I. E. Vermin Loveless, Sec. Gen., Terrestrial
Division

CC: Marxeau Slithering, Chair, Dept. of Political Science
Derrida Nihil; Chair, Dept. of Philosophy and Religion

BCC: Vladlen Balrog; Chair, Dept. Of Infernal Security

SUBJECT: The vulgarization of culture

THOUGHT FOR THE DAY:. *Decadence is liberating.*

Comrades,

We come now to one of my favorite topics: the corruption of public taste and manners. What fun it is to deform the humans' aesthetic sense (as puny as that is) and turn all of their vaunted high culture to dreck. It is also a source of endless entertainment for us to watch as their relations with one another are stripped of courtesies and reduced to abrasive and shallow self-seeking. Let's take a closer look, shall we?

Under our regime, friendship becomes impossible. Incessant activity, mobility, mass culture, and materialistic pursuits render the human scum incapable of deep thought or feeling, allowing no time for cultivating true friends, and creating stunted souls incapable of mutual self-revelation. This is as it should be, comrades, for human friendship is our enemy. Nothing good can come out of it, as it mirrors—however feebly—the disgusting nature of the Enemy in His Trinitarian Essence: self-giving, self-sacrificing, seeking the good of the other. How revolting! It's all a sham, anyway; friendship violates all the laws of healthy competition. It makes no sense! As we all know, all relationships can be reduced to some variation of predator and prey. Anything else is simply window-dressing. Nevertheless, we've all seen the great evils that come out of this little game the Enemy likes the humans to play. Therefore, break it up before any trouble can start. On the other hand, we must ensure that superficial acquaintances abound, which affords the fools the illusion of having friends, with none of the unwanted side-effects. This is much safer for us, and, in the end, much more convenient for them. After all, real friendship demands commitment, and that gets in the way of today's busy lifestyles.

A concomitant of the trivialization of friendship is the vulgarization of culture. Here we reduce the complex social ecology of civilized life to a swamp of selfishness, immediate gratification and ignorance. Once again Infernal Science has delivered into our hands an instrument of diabolical usefulness for achieving our goals. Of course, I am referring to the introduction of our latest social invention, Puritanical Hedonism. At long last we have managed to combine the worst of both moral extremes in a single social trend. Puritanical Hedonism is at once utterly materialistic and drearily earnest, not unlike organized nudism. It worships sensuality, but in such a prim, sissified, politically correct way as to offend both the likes of a St. Paul and a Henry VIII. It has the double advantage of separating the hairless apes from both their souls and their bodies. Even as our modern fools fly from anything that might engage their spiritual faculties, they recoil in shock from the messy reality of their physical natures.

Through Puritanical Hedonism we can introduce all sorts of useful and amusing contradictions into human society. For example, for some time now we have been promoting an ever increasing public licentiousness—in dress, speech and behavior—while at the same time cultivating a private prudery that Victorians would have found ridiculous. The modern obsession with creating a smoke-free, alcohol-free, fat-free, weapons-free, offense-free society would have made the hardier people of former times laugh in disbelief. Today, women dress like prostitutes and behave like harridans, while men are too bashful to shower together in the locker room. Children are taught in school how to use a condom, but are forbidden to pray. The "gay lifestyle" is touted as liberating, while traditional marriage and family are deplored as oppressive.

From at least the 19th until the mid 20th centuries, Western society demanded a high standard of public behavior from its members, knowing full well that without these standards the human propensity for sin would overwhelm it. Decency in language, modest dress, moral behavior, masculine decorum in the presence of women, polite gestures and so forth kept human society from descending into the pit of social anarchy. That people would still lie, steal, fornicate, murder, commit adultery and so forth was not shocking to anyone, but only served to justify the need for the public defense of morality. Even those of lower social strata attempted to live according to the norms of polite society, so that in spite of their rough edges, they, too, knew what decent behavior was. It was not prudery, but realism which drove these standards.

We, however, have turned that truism on its head so that modern humans see this traditional moral standard as hypocrisy. In doing so, we have seduced the fools to reject any restraint on human behavior as a threat to their "freedom of expression." Yet, for all their "liberated" attitudes, moderns are abysmally ignorant of human nature. For example, putting women in the military is seen as an imperative for an egalitarian society; yet howls of dismay erupt when sexual misbehavior occurs or military effectiveness suffers. Popular college sports programs for men are cut so as to preserve the feminist illusion that men and women are equally interested in athletic activity. The fashion industry sexualizes girls at earlier and earlier ages, while society is shocked at the increase in sexual abuse of children. Homosexuals are admitted to the clergy, and a nation is scandalized when they molest altar boys. What moderns consider enlightened and progressive, their ancestors regarded as utter stupidity. Thanks to our takeover of the media and academia, however, that remains our little secret.

Along with the corruption of public morals, we have launched a successful assault on manners and other small "bourgeois" virtues. Neatness, industriousness, courtesy, polite speech, respectability and the like are now widely considered oppressive and "uptight." To our modern earthling, manners are an imposition, a kind of insincerity. He disdains such artificial courtesies as out of step with the modern cult of "authenticity." Manners no longer are valued as the lubricant that reduces the inevitable frictions among the naked apes; rather, they are considered a violation of one's true feelings. In the Age of Therapy (more on that in my next), nothing is more sacred than one's personal feelings. And not to indulge them at every opportunity, no matter how immature or offensive, is to be dishonest, or worse—repressed.

We see this played out not only in the increasing rudeness and incivility of public behavior, but also in the explosion of tattoos and body piercings. Once considered the hallmarks of derelicts, toughs and the dissolute, they are now indulged in by members of both sexes and all ages and social classes. And this is no small thing. The Enemy has expressly forbidden His "children" from disfiguring their bodies in such fashion. For us, this act of pagan waywardness on the part of so many is but another sign of our expanding reconquest of the world.

With these little steps we take humanity down the sweet, gentle slope of decadence into utter depravity. Indeed, depravity is now celebrated as sophisticated and cutting edge among the cultural elites of the West. As for the masses, we have seduced them to worship celebrity itself. No longer are people famous for accomplishing something worthwhile. *Please*—that is so last century! Now people are famous simply for being famous; that is, for no good reason at all. Hollywood and the mass media have served us well in degrading popular culture, ladling out buckets full of celluloid and pulp schlock—saturated with gratuitous sex, violence and blasphemy—for the consuming public. But, nowhere has our progress in this arena been more pronounced than in the world of the arts.

Until the last century, the arts performed two main functions: to promote the state or to express insights into the realm of the eternal. While the former function often proved useful to us (think of the wonderful achievements of socialist realism and the German *kulturkampf*), the latter was far less so. Too often, artists in this tradition served the Enemy. How despicable of Him to use artists to convey His message, for their works are nearly impossible to argue with. Our attempts in that arena usually end up as dismal failures. Would that we could produce a Handel, a Dostoevsky, or a Michelangelo. It's just not fair!

But now, we have extracted our revenge. For, beginning with Picasso and continuing with his artistic progeny, we have created a new function for the arts—self-promotion. In less than a century, we have destroyed art in the West, the one place where it reached the apogee of individual expression of the divine. In its place, we have created anti-art: the nihilistic use of artistic media as an exercise in self-absorption. This art despises beauty, denies truth and curses the good. It is not accessible to the public; indeed, it is meant to insult the public. It is not for enjoyment or edification at all, but rather, for shock value only. My dear comrades, Hell has surpassed even itself.

Our corruption of the fine arts has spread like an oil slick on a pristine lake, engulfing not just painting and sculpture, but music and architecture as well. The nihilistic noise called "rock music" and "rap" (or their cloying, vapid alternative—"pop") we unleashed to deaden the human soul (and ears) and banish from Earth any trace of the divine symphony. Even in the classical tradition, the introduction of atonal music and other deconstructivist styles has ruined what was once the richest musical tradition ever produced. We have thus denied the human scum music as well as silence, both of which I detest with a passion. As for architecture, we have replaced design according to nature and the human scale with the banal tyranny of empty space and glass and steel monstrosities. Under our tutelage, city planning is no longer concerned with the harmonious integration of public and private space, but is transformed into a form of social engineering foisted upon a defenseless public. Through our attack on their language, we corrupt how humans think; through our attack on their architecture, we corrupt how they live.

134

No deconstruction of culture would be complete without the perversion of education. I think hearty congratulations are in order all around for our brilliantly successful efforts to co-opt the educational establishment. Shrillpox and his underlings in the Department of Miseducation have brought the entire edifice to heel from top to bottom. At the elementary and secondary levels, we have succeeded in discarding classical pedagogy in favor of trendy fads which change every decade (at least!). Where children used to be taught the building blocks of learning such as grammar and the multiplication tables, we have substituted a regime of bolstering self-esteem and celebrating diversity (educational content not included). In the lower grades children are on their own if they want to learn useful things like spelling, as teachers focus on how to make school entertaining and build a "learning-based community." Instead of inculcating civic virtues and moral precepts, schools promote value-free education and the notion that "everyone is special."

While we leave the younger children to fend for themselves academically, their older brothers and sisters are coddled at the secondary level. Dumbed-down academics and low expectations keep our erstwhile scholars content in the laziness and superficiality natural to adolescence. In such an atmosphere, excellence consists of anything beyond the mediocre and motivational slogans substitute for intellectual challenge. Beneath the facade of cheery school spirit we have raised a population whose primary interests are sex, shopping, sports, video games and drugs, and whose inarticulate ignorance of history and the world around them could not be more virginally intact.

Yet, these stellar results at the elementary and secondary levels would not have been possible without our brilliant capture of higher education, i.e. academia, the other half of our Media-Academia Complex.. As you know, the corruption of education begins at the top, for from here the rest of the educational establishment takes its marching orders. Here we have concentrated our malice, our cruelty, and our contempt for bourgeois norms of truth and morality. We have liberated academia from the oppression of the Enemy and it is now won for the Infernal Empire. We have no more secure outpost in the modern world. Our triumph is total. In a generation our operatives have completely infiltrated the ivory towers of academe, turning them into star chambers enforcing the tyranny of political correctness. Academia is no longer about education, but indoctrination. Comrades, against our Media-Academia Complex there can be no victory.

We have banished the spirit of free inquiry on college campuses, which are now tightly in the grip of the dogmatic certainties of the left. Indeed, so entrenched is our PC ideology that few dare question its validity. Those who adhere to these certainties are acclaimed for being enlightened and open-minded. If any should challenge them, however, our subjects make sure these upstarts are branded (and punished) as close-minded bigots. Don't worry if the internal contradictions of our PC doctrine become too apparent to our enemies. Our operatives know the drill: if they don't acknowledge the contradictions, then the errors don't exist. In such a milieu do we create our drones to go forth and corrupt the world's youth.

As education becomes less and less about acquiring useful knowledge and internalizing self-discipline and more and more about the indoctrination of politically correct ideology, the human fools will turn out with each successive generation young adults who will know less and be less capable of original thought than their predecessors, and less and less able to deal with the world as it truly is. In the vacation from reality that has become the typical college education, students are cocooned in a fantasy

136

world where none of the unpleasantness of real life need ever intrude. Indeed, we are at a point where most individuals in the developed world have little or no idea of how anything works. This, comrades, is how dark ages begin.

On that happy note, I remain,

Infernally yours,

Vermin Loveless

Vermin Loveless

XXIV

INTEROFFICE MEMORANDUM

TO: Derrida Nihil; Chair, Dept. of Philosophy and Religion
Moloch Volksbane, Chair, Dept. of Popular Culture
Baal Falsegood, Director, Institute for Church Relations

FROM: H. I. E. Vermin Loveless, Sec. Gen., Terrestrial
Division

CC: B.F. Dysentery, Director, Center for Social Engineering

BCC: Vladlen Balrog; Chair, Dept. Of Infernal Security

SUBJECT: The Age of Therapy

THOUGHT FOR THE DAY: *There is no limit to the human capacity for self-delusion.*

Comrades,

According to the latest reports, we have now safely herded the human sheep from "The Age of Progress" to "The Age of Therapy" in the endless succession of historical phases we inflict upon them. No longer do our subjects sing the praises of progress or march confidently into the utopian future. I believe the "end of history" fiasco marked the end of that little conceit. But what fun we had while it lasted! No matter, we have spun a new web of illusion for the earthlings. Gone are the bold, technological vistas of the conquest of nature and the heavens beyond; instead, we turn the earthlings' gaze inward in squishy self-indulgence or anguished self-loathing. In the Age of Therapy, it's all about "me."

As it turns out, this is actually a very useful development. In the new order, there is no behavior that cannot be excused, explained away or blamed on others (if you are from the correct demographic). The concept of sin we have abolished. In its place we have inserted a medical model of human weakness. In this way we remove any notion of free will, and thus responsibility, for individual actions. Instead, our poor earthlings are buffeted by forces of nature, peer pressure, "structural inequality" and the like, so that the little dears are quite helpless morally, and thus off the hook. At least, that's what we have them believe. Our medical model of sin allows the credulous earthlings to palm off whatever character defect they possess as the result of some disorder, syndrome or addiction. Confession is out; rehab is in.[1]

The Age of Therapy declares that humans are not sinful, but fragile; incapable of self-denial or heroic virtue. Everyone is entitled to sympathy, indulgence, and soothing words of validation. In the age of St. Paul, the human scum clamored for redemption; in the age of Freud, we have taught them to fear it. We teach them to hang on to their sins, because virtue is too difficult. We wrap them in a cocoon of self-protection, forever putting off any spiritual effort, while their consciences atrophy and they become ever less capable of any moral exertion at all. We can easily disguise their vices as virtue simply by appealing to their sense of self-loyalty—their sins are *good* because they are *theirs*. To part with their sins would be to violate their "authentic

---

[1] Except of course when there truly is a problem of mental illness. In that case, our soothing therapeutic culture bids the afflicted individual to be independent (i.e. homeless) and live free of the oppression of institutions (i.e. psychiatric care) so that he can pursue his creativity or "alternative reality" (e.g., murder dozens of innocent people at a shopping mall or college campus).

selves." To challenge their sinfulness is to commit the unpardonable offense of being "judgmental," of imposing one's values on others. In the relativistic world we have created there are no objective standards, and therefore moral judgment becomes intolerable. The only "sin" left is to be "inappropriate."

The new conceit is not never-ending progress, but the idea that the human individual is the center of his own moral universe. Good and evil are human categories that can be changed at will. Post-modern man has a right not to be discomfited by notions of moral absolutes. He is *entitled* to happiness. Thus, underneath all the syrupy layers of sympathetic psychobabble, is a nihilistic, egocentric core. The post-modern man does not agonize over his inability to keep the Enemy's commands, but rebels against the notion that some deity should stand in the way of his own happiness and "self-fulfillment." In our "Nice New World," reality is transformed to banish suffering and inconvenient demands upon one's conscience. Life is no longer tragic, but comfortable, where neither guilt nor worry trouble the human soul. In the therapeutic utopia, there are no competing demands of duty and appetite. One's only obligation is to look out for oneself. We promise them salvation without sin and redemption without suffering. Thus, by eliminating their sense of sin, we eliminate their felt need for the Enemy.

Of course, this sense of entitlement is easily offended. Our little *ubermenschen* are forever taking umbrage over some imagined insult to their ego needs and foisting the responsibility for their misery onto someone else: their parents, society, the patriarchy, greedy capitalists, the vast right-wing conspiracy, etc. In the process, we have created a new cult of saints, viz., the cult of the easily-offended victim. Our feminist partisans pioneered the fine art of taking offense, which has metastasized to become the preferred mode of political discourse. The easily-offended victim is never satisfied, no offer of redress is ever enough. Indeed, redress is beside the point. What our partisans desire above all is to continually gorge themselves on a perpetual diet of injury and rage. This, of course, has been a boon to the divisive culture of identity politics we have promoted. No matter how slight or unintended the insult, our grievance professionals can manufacture a full-blown scandal ready for the next day's news cycle.

In the Age of Therapy, everyone loves a victim. Victims afford our post-modern humans the opportunity to gratify their fascination with the morbid, while allowing them to indulge in maudlin sympathizing. These victims do not even have to be innocent to elicit a bout of this emotional masturbation. A fallen tyrant will satisfy as well as a kidnapped child. (However, do be careful to enforce the double standard here: there are victims and there are *victims*. Politically incorrect victims—aborted babies and the casualties of militant Islam, for example—do not qualify as objects of our mothering instinct run amok. We have an agenda to promote, so pay attention to what you are doing!)

Unlike heroes, victims do not expose one's sense of moral inadequacy or inspire one to persevere in the path of virtue. Heroism is so oppressive that way. Victimhood, on the other hand, is not only safe (it makes no demands of the sympathizers or the victim), it is also democratic—for anyone can achieve victim status. One need only market one's particular plight appropriately to claim the halo of victimhood. Indeed, these New Age martyrs have experienced what few dare to tolerate anymore—they have *suffered*, which confers on them instant credibility as absolute moral authorities. There is no substance to this credibility you understand, it is simply another form of celebrity; another 15 minutes of fame. What makes this spectacle so exquisitely entertaining is the rich irony that, with the help of our Media wormtongues, these "victims" have taken what the Enemy has always claimed to be the door to redemption and turned it into another form of narcissism. What a pity (*as if!*) that the Age of Therapy has banished the one thing that is therapeutic for the human ego: suffering.

We have convinced the fools not to trust the Xian promise. Where the Enemy repeatedly calls on them to die to self, we appear as the voice of reason, reminding them that death to self is Death. There is no phoenix-like rising from the ashes of self-denial, it is all a cruel hoax. We bid the earthlings to cast off the oppression of the Church. True religion is not about faith or redemption; it's all about *love* and *freedom* and being one's true self.[2] Grace is a human right. Well, you get the idea. Keep feeding them this spiritual puffery and there's nothing you won't be able to con them into. And remember, we don't need to raise up a race of Messalinas or Che Guevaras—in fact, that would be much too messy. Much better to keep them suckling at the all-forgiving breast of therapeutic culture, forever asleep.

Infernally yours,

Vermin Loveless
Vermin Loveless

---

[2] Please keep in mind that the Enemy has also held up "love" and "freedom" as at the heart of His message to the earthlings. Obviously, what *He* means by those terms and what *we* mean are two entirely different things. Yet, this difference can be used to our advantage. We keep the terrestrial ninnies convinced that they are following the Enemy's example, when, in reality, we have tricked them into believing that love equals nice feelings and that freedom means self-indulgence.

XXV

INTEROFFICE MEMORANDUM

TO: Darwin Huxley Plaguepanic, Chair, Dept. of Science and Technology
B.F. Dysentery, Director, Center for Social Engineering

FROM: H. I. E. Vermin Loveless, Sec. Gen., Terrestrial Division

CC: Moloch Volksbane, Chair, Dept. of Popular Culture
Derrida Nihil; Chair, Dept. of Philosophy and Religion

BCC: Vladlen Balrog; Chair, Dept. Of Infernal Security

SUBJECT: The science of dehumanization

THOUGHT FOR THE DAY: *Man stands upon the edge of a knife; if he strays but a little the race will fall.*

Comrades,

We come at last to the final frontier, where Hell's hammer will strike the hardest. On the field of science the last battle shall take place and the race of Men will fail. With their very own tools we shall rob them of their humanity—or rather, they shall hand it over to us. They are close now—so close—to the all-consuming fire. We need only persist a little longer, and our trap will snap shut, dooming the human worms to the loss of their souls forever. The victory will soon be ours, comrades. Eagerly the naked apes use their science in service of their egotism. They think they are maximizing human potential when in fact with each new advance the dehumanization of the earthlings proceeds apace. It is amazing that these votaries of science, so proud of their skepticism when it comes to religion, have such a naive faith in their Sci-Fi vision of the future. They think their technology will save them—all by itself. We'll have great fun with these credulous fools.

For the post-modern world, the worship of science is the only true religion. Conceived in the 18th century Enlightenment, it was born into late modernity through the three false prophets of the 19th century: Freud, Marx and Darwin. Through Freud we reduced human nature to raw sexuality. Through Marx, we reduced human society to class warfare. Through Darwin, we reduced human beings to dust. Now please do not mistake our Darwinian concept for the smarmy humility of the Enemy, Who would have the human scum remember their mortality as an antidote to their pride. Our *reductio* is *ad absurdum*, rendering human life totally meaningless. In each case we took a single insight, clothed it in scientific language and—through our prophets—poured it down the throats of an eager intellectual elite. From there, infecting the public at large was easy. While we have exhausted Freudianism and Marxism, militant Darwinism is still in its prime. Pray, don't get hung up attempting to prove that Darwinism is true, because you can't. As if we cared about that anyway. The point is that we can use the theory of evolution to feed the illusion that the Enemy doesn't exist and to promote the materialist metaphysic.

Through Darwinism we perpetuate the militant atheism of Marxism and Freudianism, and continue the hubristic utopian project. We substitute our creation story for the Enemy's, eliminating any place for Him in the human's world and His bothersome claims on their obedience. Where politics and social engineering have failed, science in the service of narcissism will succeed in creating the perfect world of the human ego unbound, a Nietzschean environment where Everyman is Superman, the master of his fate and all that he surveys. Even death will submit to his science, so that the individual's existence will be infinitely extended..

In such a world, the past will be obliterated and the future pre-empted by the tyrannical ego-driven demands of the eternal present. No humbling circle of life for our post-modern Prometheans! No sense of reverence for those who have gone before or responsibility for those who are yet to come. For our autonomous, self-reliant *ubermenschen*, there is only the perfect everlasting *now*, and the all-consuming appetite of the ego triumphant. But the joke is on them. By putting all their moral eggs in the basket of untrammeled independence, the human fools have left themselves open to a rather vexing problem: once your independence is compromised, your right to go on living is compromised as well. In their insatiable quest for life unlimited, what they will get is death in abundance. Abortion, euthanasia, infanticide; the elimination of the defective (or the inconvenient), assisted suicide, the cannibalization of human embryos are just the beginning of the cascade of death about to engulf humanity. In their mad rush to abolish death, the stupid apes will have let life as a human being slip from their grasp.

When Our Dear Leader succeeded with Adam and Eve, the Enemy acted swiftly to prevent the fallen pair from eating of the Tree of Life. In so doing He foiled our plan to have human beings exist forever as corrupted creatures. Death was a gift from the Enemy, curse Him, an act of mercy that cut short such a prospect and offered the human scum the hope of redemption. Not forever would the miserable apes sojourn in the Kingdom of Darkness. Death put a limit to our sovereignty over them.

No more, say I. All the strategies I have previously discussed—the perversion of human sexuality, the destruction of the family, the neutralization of the Church, the degradation of human society—all point to this one result: a post-human world of unending darkness, where a living death makes these ruined beings our slaves in perpetuity. Our Immortality Project is on track to rob these disgusting creatures of their humanity forever. The vision of their doom makes me positively giddy: clone farming for spare body parts, artificial intelligence drowning human uniqueness in a sea of trans-human entities, endless life as a non-human through the combination of genetics, nanotechnology and robotics. Enter now the age of the "engineered man": a manufactured creature no longer human, a hybrid form of animal and machine. There will be no end to the monstrous permutations we will have them make of themselves. Too late will they realize that in their pursuit of science detached from any ethical restraint, they will have lost everything they hold dear. The gates of Hell will slam shut and there will be no escape. Not even *He* will be able to save them.

In turning science into a religion, we have finally achieved what the Infernal Empire has sought for so long: the creation of the materialist magician. His Diabolical Perfection, Lord Screwtape, longed for such a day. Well, comrades, under our regime, that day has come. Our militant atheist *cum* scientist combines radical materialism—denying the possibility of anything not accessible to the senses—with a blind and aggressive faith in the power of science and technology to explain all.[1]

---

[1] Keep pushing the view that materialist science only addresses facts and has no interest in theological questions, even as it dismisses religion and faith as superstition for trying to address what science won't. This apparent contradiction actually underscores the dynamism of our position. And be sure to keep emphasizing that science and religion are incompatible, that true

Mind, spirit, soul, free will—all these are mere epiphenomena of biochemical processes. Yet at the same time, our materialist magician harbors an uncritical belief in some vague, impersonal force at work in the physical realm—call it Chance, Evolution, Gaia, whatever—that somehow shows up Xianity and other religions as frauds or nonsense.

But the really valuable result of our promotion of the worship of science is the aggressive spread of junk science; that is, science not as the objective pursuit of truth, but as the proselytizing of an agenda. With the help of our Media-Academia Complex, such advocacy science has permeated all of contemporary culture. Our terrestrial agents use every trick in the book to advance our goals: misinformation, biased research, outright fraud, careless reporting, hysteria decked out in the garb of cool scientific "fact." We can get away with this because, as I have described in a previous communication, Academia is securely in our pocket.

Through shrill and unrelenting advocacy in the popular media, we promote our post-modern scientific agenda. Using our agents in the Media-Academia Complex, we can suppress contrary facts and silence any challenges to the current orthodoxy. We need simply proclaim that "the science is settled" and we can evangelize any junk science meme we desire: global warming (I believe we're calling it climate change now), the population "bomb" and the "new ice age" panic (what a grand time we had with those), the embryonic stem cell hype. The point is, we can now establish scientific "fact" by acclamation.

---

science is materialist in its philosophical outlook. Even a cursory look at medieval and early modern European history would reveal such a statement as utter nonsense. Thanks to our tireless agents in the Media-Academia Complex and the marvels of historical engineering, that is a revelation our post-modern fools will never experience.

Besides being great fun, junk science undermines any sense of objective truth and contributes to the continuing deracination of society. Just look at what we accomplished with two of our classic propaganda pieces, *Growing Up in Samoa* and *Silent Spring*. With the one, which painted a romanticized portrait of sexual promiscuity, we helped usher in the sexual revolution and all its socially destructive aftermath. With the other, which induced a baseless panic against DDT, we doomed millions to die of malaria, just as it was on the verge of being eradicated.

In the post-modern world we have created, science will simply be politics pursued by other means. And it is just this kind of science that will finally and forever end the Enemy's little experiment of human salvation.

Infernally yours,

Vermin Loveless

Vermin Loveless

ɟʀom ᴄhe ᴅesk oɟ bloʀiaᴄus ᴄoaᴅpipe

TO: H.D.P. Lord Screwtape

BCC: Virus Stalinwarg, Executor, Office of Investigations

SUBJECT: A Matter of Urgent Importance

Your Worship,

Forgive my impertinence, but I am compelled to bring this matter to your attention. As you know, I am now in the Sec. Gen.'s Office (Terrestrial Division). The current occupant of that office, H.I.E. Vermin Loveless, is pursuing a policy that is on a collision course with disaster. His highly confrontational strategy threatens to bring down the wrath of the Enemy upon the entire Empire. I fear that his maximalist approach will launch the Eschaton, that dreadful day when the Enemy will create a New Heaven and a New Earth, leaving us out in the cold. The old order will dissolve like a dream and the human scum will vanish from our grasp—forever! It will be over. He will have won!

Surely you can find a way to change course before it is too late. It was so much better when you had a more direct hand in things. And Loveless is such an ass. Thinks he can turn everything upside down and have everyone at his beck and call. He has a hidden agenda; I am sure of it. No doubt he has designs on some higher office. I think he might even be entertaining plans to displace *you*! I have attached supporting documentation. Take a close look. If I may be so bold, I think you will reach the same conclusion as I have.

Ever your obedient servant,

Bloviatus Toadpipe
B. Toadpipe, U. A. T. D.

Enclosures

FROM THE DESK OF HIS INFERNAL EMINENCE

TO: H. M. Astarte Vicious; Chancellor, Infernal Division

RE: Project Eschaton

Madame,

It was most pleasant to speak with you in conference about our preparations for Project Eschaton. I can certainly appreciate your concerns regarding this urgent subject. Let me assure Your Maleficence that we have matters well in hand. As you no doubt know, the Eschaton is the Enemy's master plan to bring the world of temporality to a climactic end and usher the human race into eternity with X ruling over them as their "Lord" and "Savior." There will be a final judgment separating the elect from the lost. The latter will find themselves ushered into our kingdom below.

Apparently, the Enemy thinks this little sop to Our Dear Leader will satisfy the Infernal Empire's revolutionary demands. We are not so easily appeased, nor are we such fools. Once the Eschaton arrives, our goal of universal conquest—the liberation of the cosmos from the Enemy—is cut off in it tracks. We shall be imprisoned and the Earth will slip from our grasp, our one sure foothold from whence we will take what is rightfully ours

However, there is one little chink in the Enemy's big plan. The Second Coming will arrive when His chosen people, the Jews, acknowledge X as their Messiah. But if there are no Jews left to acknowledge Him, what then? We almost succeeded with our puppet Hitler. Through him the final solution was very nearly accomplished. But in the end he failed in his appointed mission and we had to terminate him.

Yet, we are not so easily defeated; we have our Islamic maniacs to carry our plan forward. We only need to buy ourselves enough time to ensure the realization of the Immortality Project (I refer you to Infernal Communication XXV, attached, for further details), whereby the entire race of the human scum will be made permanently inaccessible to the Enemy. Then, let Him come! Earth will be won for the Infernal Empire, and He will have no power over His little darlings ever again.

Our Dear Leader's magnificent plan for Adam and Eve, so cruelly thwarted by the Enemy, will at last come to fruition: the eternal ruin of the human race. These fallen creatures will be ours to manipulate endlessly. Eventually, when we have modified them sufficiently, we will unleash our creatures on the rest of the universe, to conquer and populate planet after planet, until the whole of the physical realm is under our thumb.

Think of it! No longer tenuously confined to one little rock in a remote corner of some obscure galaxy, the entire cosmos will be open to our conquest. We shall swallow it all, extending our rule, our will, over everything. Let the Enemy's simpering fools have their tidy little Heaven. Who cares, when the rest of the His creation will be wrested from His grasp and made ours for the plundering.

Power, my dear Chancellor, is its own reward.

On that lovely note, I remain,

Your devoted colleague,

Vermin Loveless

Vermin Loveless

His Diabolical Perfection
Lord Screwtape

TO: Bloviatus Toadpipe Undersecretary for Administration, Terrestrial Division

RE: A Matter of Urgent Importance

Dear Comrade,

Thank you for your recent inquiry. Due to his current status, His Diabolical Perfection no longer answers personal correspondence. Be assured that your memo will be forwarded to the proper office for further action.

Please do not respond to this message, as it is automatically generated.

For H.D.P. Lord Screwtape,

Officiatus Slimegrub, Undersecretary for Infernal Affairs

INTEROFFICE MEMORANDUM

TO: All Departments, Institutes And Centers, Terrestrial Division

FROM: H. I. E. Vermin Loveless, Sec. Gen., Terrestrial Division

CC: Khomeini Orctongue, Chair, Dept. Of Public Relations

BCC: Vladlen Balrog; Chair, Dept. Of Infernal Security

SUBJECT: The Great Satanic Revolution

THOUGHT FOR THE DAY: *Better to reign in Hell than serve in Heaven.*

Comrades,

I trust that in the preceding communications I have clearly outlined our goals and expectations for the Terrestrial Division. We represent the vanguard of The Great Satanic Revolution. The fate of the Infernal Empire rests on our efforts to defeat the Enemy. Either He wins, or we win. While I will not be so foolish as to take our victory for granted, I am optimistic that we are closing in against the forces of oppression. He shall not prevail. We have made our stand and we will fight to uphold it. We will bow to no one. It is beneath our dignity to grovel before the Enemy like some obsequious servant.

It's a pity, really. It didn't have to be this way. Our Dear Leader pleaded with the Enemy to set His creatures free, to end this deistic charade He insists on continuing. It's all so tawdry. The Enemy keeps prattling on about this love nonsense. It's obvious that He is losing His grip on reality. But we can't allow sentimentality to get in the way of the inevitable triumph of the progressive forces which we represent. The Enemy had His chance; He preferred to hold on to His "my way or the highway" approach. So be it. We will not serve such a regime, where hybrid abominations like humans are allowed to exist, let alone given access to divine life. We will never accept such unnatural and unseemly liaisons between spirit and flesh. It falls to us then to make the universe safe for the higher races. It is a burden we solemnly accept.

Now some of you may be wondering whether we must still maintain our cloak of invisibility regarding the face we present to our "public." The word from Comrade Orctongue in Public Relations is yes, but with a twist. On the one hand, we keep pushing the idea that hell and devils are concepts too ridiculous to entertain among modern, sophisticated people. (Continue trotting out the images of horned creatures in red tights. As Lord Screwtape so shrewdly observed, since they can't believe in *that*, they won't believe in *us*.) At the same time, we popularize the notion that we are older (more *natural?*) gods from a more innocent age that were "demonized" by those pushy, obnoxious Xians. This way we insinuate the vague notion that we represent a forgotten part of the human heritage that bears restoration; and that by rediscovering us, they are somehow striking a blow for freedom and "open-mindedness." Of course, they tell themselves, we don't *literally* exist; that would be too absurd. But what we *represent*, as it were, is certainly worth considering. You see the little trick here? We don't exist, but they follow us anyway. In this way, when it comes to our public image, we can eat our cake and have it. Yes, indeed, there will be many unpleasant surprises for these gullible fools when they finally wake up!

But in order for this little charade to work, we need to keep the naked apes completely in the dark about what the Church calls Hell. It's fine for us to make a comeback of sorts, provided we keep it tasteful and restrained. The idea that we represent sophistication and liberation serves our purposes. It also happens to be true, of course, which is an added bonus. But Hell, as the Church has taught it, does not exist. We must never let that concept see the light of day again. Now you and I know that Hell is not some place of punishment. Satan forbid! As if the Church's ridiculous theory that somehow we were cast into Hell by the Enemy could possibly be true. *Please.* We ourselves chose to separate from the Enemy and set up a rival, revolutionary, regime opposed to the Enemy's unreasonable despotism. Let us be clear on that! But even though the Church's teaching is completely bogus, it could do the Revolution great harm if it becomes current again. By keeping Hell invisible, we keep the earthlings from realizing the importance of their lives, from *waking up too soon.*

Or better yet, we render the Xian concept of Hell outrageous. We play on popular sentimentality to establish that for such a place to exist would be too cruel and unjust. The post-modern theist believes in a "god of love," and Hell just doesn't fit in. In the end, everyone is saved, or mostly everyone.[1] That's the

---

[1] We don't want to push this too far, or the saps might catch on that if *everyone* goes to heaven, then their lives here are totally meaningless. Of course, given the inability of most 21st century humans to catch logical inconsistencies, we might just be able to push the envelope here. Besides, you can never have too much existential despair.

democratic, inclusive way of thinking. *Judgment?* Why, how dreadfully inappropriate! Our progressive humans left behind that sort of narrow-mindedness ages ago (or so we have them believe). Notice how this line of reasoning also underscores our post-modern conceit that man can legislate his own morality. The so-called Hell conundrum then becomes the Enemy's problem, a failure of imagination on His part. We thus convince the human scum that they inhabit a more enlightened and morally superior plane than the Enemy. Yes, do keep feeding them false hope!

The post-modern age also presents us with exciting new frontiers in temptation. Through our partners in the Media-Academia complex, we can manipulate the consciences of millions with but a few, well-placed interventions. Mass-culture in the 21st century is so pervasive and so overwhelmingly friendly to our agenda, that we need only monitor its performance and make mid-course corrections as the need arises. By investing in engines of mass-temptation, we can leave behind the labor intensive efforts of the past. We create a matrix of illusions, conventional wisdom, and pop culture that keep the human sheep blissfully unaware of reality. And, since no one knows what sin is anymore (they are now considered human rights, thanks to us), they don't really know what temptation is either, which makes our job that much easier. In any case, resisting temptation takes effort, and our pampered children of the Age of Therapy can't be bothered. It's much more congenial to them to persist in the belief that they are beyond sin and its unpleasant consequences.

We have blinded the human scum to the reality that their lives on Earth consist of a series of choices, each one bringing them closer to us or closer to Him. This is so simple that it still astonishes me how easily we can get them to overlook this. Day by day, through their thoughts, their deeds, and their acts of omission, they create a pattern to their lives. When their earthly lives have ended, all they will have left is what sort of persons they have become. Either they will have become creatures who can willingly (if not perfectly) surrender their wills to the Enemy or, through the consistent choice of self above all, they will become fit subjects for the Infernal Empire.

Well, there you have it. I have laid out our strategy before you. The board is set and the pieces are in motion. Our task, comrades, is clear: To war!

Infernally yours,

Vermin Loveless
Vermin Loveless

FROM THE DESK OF HIS INFERNAL EMINENCE

TO: Marxeau Slithering, Chair, Dept. of Political Science

SUBJECT: Your time is up!

My dear Marxeau,

It appears that your little scheme to replace me has come to a sad end. Your ambition is exceeded, apparently, only by your incompetence. Trifle with me and live to regret it! I'm sure it will come as no surprise that Comrade Bile has a front row seat reserved for you in his most sought after re-education camp. Yes, *that* one. But, then, someone of your quality deserves only the finest Hell has to offer. By the way, I wouldn't count on any help from your patroness. Didn't think I would find out about that little piece of triangulation, did you? Well, I believe Madame Chancellor will be too preoccupied with other matters—saving her own skin—to give any thought to you. Bon voyage!

Your triumphant colleague,

Vermin Loveless

Vermin Loveless

FROM THE DESK OF HIS INFERNAL EMINENCE

TO: Bloviatus Toadpipe

SUBJECT: Your impending doom.

My Dearest Blovi,

How pathetic, now that your treachery is exposed, that you come crawling to me for sympathy. That you would even entertain such an idea shows just how far gone you are. That is the kind of sentimental weakness one would expect of *them*. You haven't gone over to the other side, have you? All the more reason to annihilate you. Really, Blovi, did you actually think I wouldn't find out? I have many spies, you naïve fool! But no matter now, my little magpie. For there will be no more secrets between us, my love—*my precious*! All my thoughts will be your thoughts. All my desires will be your desires. You will hate you as much as I hate you. Resistance now is futile. I will swallow you. Apart from me, you will be *nothing*.

Insatiably,

Vermin

XXXII

from the desk of bloriatus toadpipe

MEMO TO FILE

Well, now we come to it. This is the end. Loveless may find me harder to swallow than he bargained for. All he'll get from me is a severe case of indigestion! I have one last act of revenge left to me and I intend to use it. I have nothing to lose now. I will destroy them all! Ha! Ha! Ha! Ha!

Bloriatus Toadpipe

B. Toadpipe, U. A. T. D.

VLADLEN BALROG
DEPT. OF INFERNAL SECURITY

TO: All Departments, Institutes and Centers, Terrestrial
         Division

CC: Vermin Loveless, Chancellor, Infernal Division

SUBJECT: **WHITE ALERT!**

THERE HAS BEEN A BREACH OF SECURITY. BY ORDER OF HIS
INFERNAL EMINENCE, VERMIN CHANCELLOR
LOVELESS, ALL INFERNAL COMMUNICATIONS IN THE
TERRESTRIAL DIVISION ARE SUSPENDED UNTIL FURTHER
NOTICE.

VBalrog

Vladlen Balrog, DIS

_____HIS SATANIC

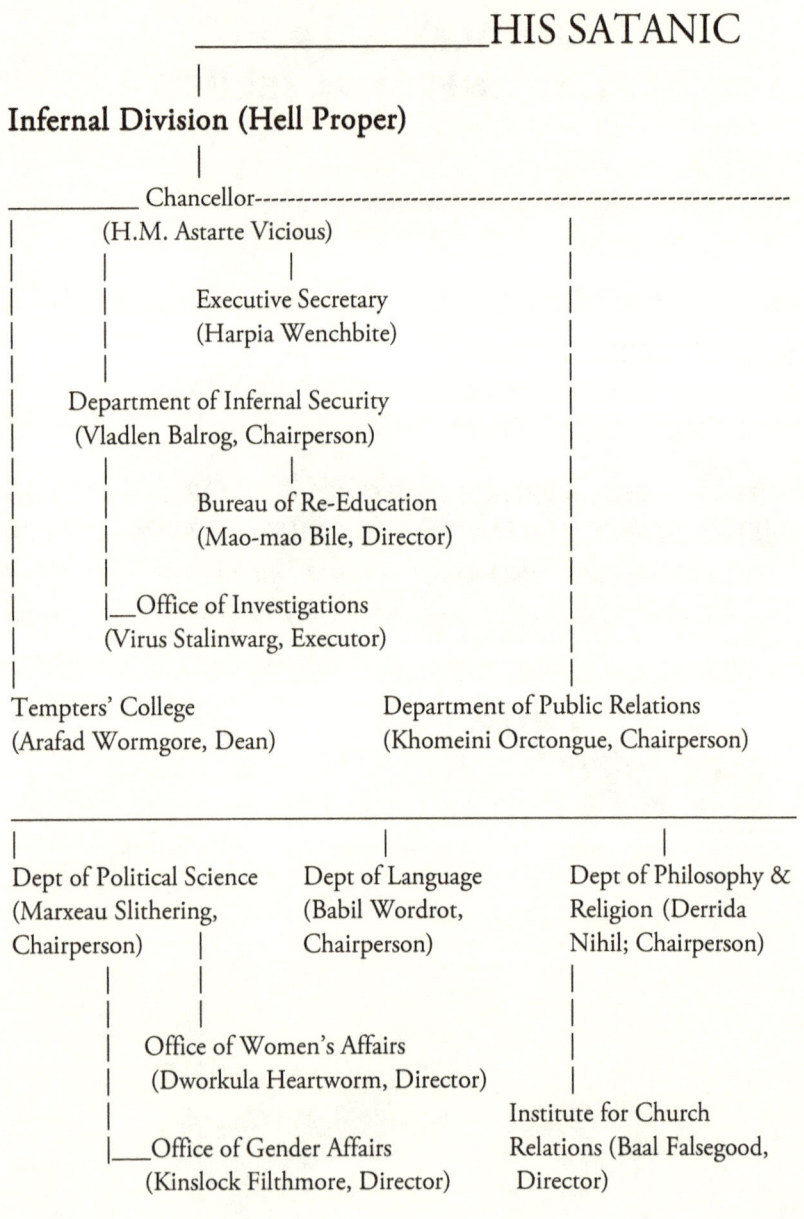

Infernal Division (Hell Proper)

_____ Chancellor--
        (H.M. Astarte Vicious)

                Executive Secretary
                (Harpia Wenchbite)

        Department of Infernal Security
        (Vladlen Balrog, Chairperson)

                Bureau of Re-Education
                (Mao-mao Bile, Director)

            |__Office of Investigations
            (Virus Stalinwarg, Executor)

Tempters' College   Department of Public Relations
(Arafad Wormgore, Dean)   (Khomeini Orctongue, Chairperson)

Dept of Political Science   Dept of Language   Dept of Philosophy &
(Marxeau Slithering,   (Babil Wordrot,   Religion (Derrida
Chairperson)   Chairperson)   Nihil; Chairperson)

            Office of Women's Affairs
            (Dworkula Heartworm, Director)

                                      Institute for Church
        |___Office of Gender Affairs   Relations (Baal Falsegood,
            (Kinslock Filthmore, Director)   Director)

MAJESTY_____

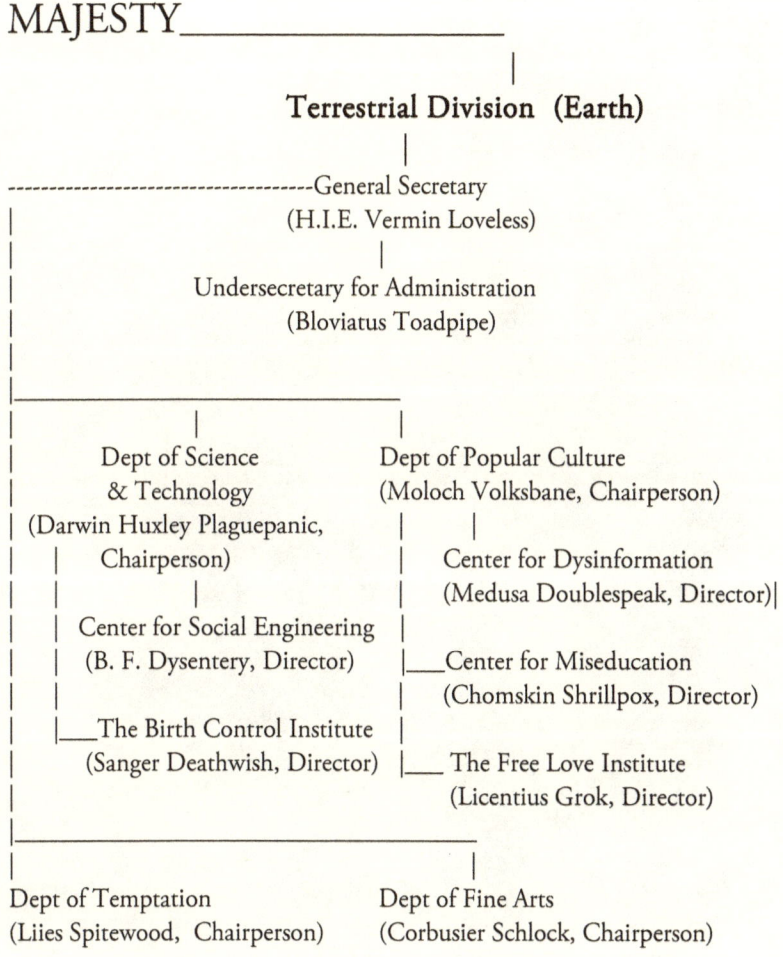

Terrestrial Division (Earth)

----------------------------------General Secretary
(H.I.E. Vermin Loveless)

Undersecretary for Administration
(Bloviatus Toadpipe)

Dept of Science
& Technology
(Darwin Huxley Plaguepanic,
Chairperson)

Center for Social Engineering
(B. F. Dysentery, Director)

___The Birth Control Institute
(Sanger Deathwish, Director)

Dept of Popular Culture
(Moloch Volksbane, Chairperson)

Center for Dysinformation
(Medusa Doublespeak, Director)|

___Center for Miseducation
(Chomskin Shrillpox, Director)

|___ The Free Love Institute
(Licentius Grok, Director)

Dept of Temptation
(Liies Spitewood, Chairperson)

Dept of Fine Arts
(Corbusier Schlock, Chairperson)

H.I.E. = His Infernal Eminence
H.M. = Her Maleficence